The Deepwater Trilogy

Deepwater Black
Deepwater Landing
Deepwater Angels

Deepwater Angels

Ken Catran

Hodder
Children's
Books

a division of Hodder Headline plc

For Wendy

Contents

Prologue

Deepwater is the name of a spaceship, built and launched on Mars in the last decade of the twenty-first century. It was designed to cross the universe, so its teenage crew is very special. No ordinary crew could endure the impossible distances and time-spans they would have to travel; so this crew was cloned from gene cells on the spaceship and grew up under the care of a super bio-computer called NUN. Until their second round-universe journey ended on Earth, they had no life other than Deepwater.

Because they were cloned from gene cells, they have a special problem. Every gene has a built-in slice of the previous memory of the person from whom the gene cell was taken. They live this memory like a time trip. They call this 'pre-existing,' shortened to 'prexing'. So Deepwater's teenage crew live two lives; on the spaceship and that section of a past life.

Deepwater is a gene ark, its mission to restore life to the dead planet of Earth, as recounted in *Deepwater Black*. The second mission was to recover the human gene bank from the other Deepwater, wrecked on the far shores of the universe; then, fighting off unknown and terrible dangers, to return to Earth – as told in *Deepwater Landing,* when the spaceship crashlands on the new living Earth.

There are eight gene caskets on Deepwater and only seven have opened. The last is still closed; Deepwater has crashed on Earth and the human gene bank has yet to operate.

Can it be operated? Is the mission finished? Deepwater has circled the universe twice, but does adventure still wait? The teenage crew were only selectively taught about the powers of.their spaceship by their bio-computer teacher, NUN. They don't know why the eighth casket is still closed. Or when it will open.

In *Deepwater Black,* an Earth-boy, Robbie, found himself caught in the teenage body of a Deepwater crew-person. In *Deepwater Landing,* the Earth-girl, Denie Miles, is on Deepwater spaceship. But now, the whole enormous whale-length of Deepwater seems to be stranded forever – when the eighth casket opens.

Robbie knew Denie and they both knew the school bully, Connal Burkitt – Meatgrinder – who made their lives a misery when he could. But Connal had pressures they didn't understand; nor did they realise how linked he was to them. That the eighth casket would begin another adventure is even more awesome.

Connal Burkitt is the eighth crew-person. *Deepwater Angels* is his story.

1 Palace of the vampires

I was on the run from the cops when all this started. Not many kids get chased for major jewel thefts, but I was. I hadn't done anything and it wasn't Mum's fault, either, because Roger had just shown up out of nowhere. He was an old mate of my dad's, he said, and Mum knows I like meeting these people. So she let him stay for a few days. The problem was (we found out later) that every night Roger was crashing his van through jewellers' windows and cleaning out their showcases. He was what the cops call a 'ramraider', and very good at his job.

After a couple of days, I knew that something was wrong. Roger had this heavy knapsack that stayed strapped tight and he always sat up when the crime news came on telly. But he could tell me all kinds of stories about Dad, so I liked him. And the day the cops came, he slung the bag to me and hissed sharply 'Run!'

I did run, not just for him, but because Mum might get into trouble too. Out the back, on to my bike and down the road, just ahead of a cop car coming round the corner.

I had a good place to hide. In the park and bushland near our school is an old storm-drain. I stashed the bag first, under a footbridge that Denie Miles once booby-trapped to throw me and Reeboks into the muddy creek. Then I went to a dairy to get some crisps, ice-cream and sausages.

Hiding out is not as easy as it looks in the movies. I ate the chips and got a fire started from twigs. But the sausages just burned and by the time I'd eaten them, the ice-cream

3

had melted. And I was really worried because the cops might be looking for me now. I had nobody to help me but Reeboks, my best friend, and I wasn't sure he'd get on the wrong side of the law for me. Even if I had to live in this storm-drain a long time, it was better than Mum going to jail.

Nothing happened for about an hour. It was Friday of a long weekend, so I had until Tuesday before school started looking for me, too. Ms Booth, our teacher, is even worse than the cops for sniffing out trouble. I was sad when I realised I might have to leave school. I used to heavy the other kids, but Denie Miles stopped me doing that and didn't treat me like a thicko, either. I had nothing to think about, so tried to imagine myself in a video game. I'm good at these and my favourite is Torkan the Awesome. So I sat in the tunnel, shut my eyes and tried to imagine Torkan where I had left him, in the pit of the tiger spiders.

Then it happened. All the light somehow went and everything spun. And instead of sitting cross-legged, I was suddenly lying down and there was a glittery darkness above – and that made me even *more* scared, because the glitterdarkness was shaped like a coffin-lid of thick, light-twinkling glass.

I was in a big grey room, as huge as a football field. There were two big doors at either end and I looked round. I was inside a long, coffin-shaped box and there were seven more, three still closed. I knew straightaway what'd happened because I'd seen films about kids getting sucked into video games and fantasy worlds. It'd happened to me, too, when I'd played one video game or read one comic too many and somehow zapped myself into a cosmic fantasy world. It didn't look like *Torkan in the Cave of Creeping Cobwebs,* but four of those coffins were open and four against one was too much.

In this fantasy world, I had nothing on but a silver-grey track suit – not even a helmet or sword. I jumped out of the coffin, decided not to hang around and headed for the nearest door. I had to get out of this place before a vampire sank its teeth into my neck. So I staggered through the big archway at the end and over a black floor that bounced like a water-bed. Then down a long winding tunnel with lots of holes set in the walls, some gleaming with crystals. This wasn't swords and fantasy stuff, as there were no skeletons, chains and dungeons. It was more like science-fiction and space-age vampires, but they were just as deadly.

Now there was a round tunnel ahead with doors set in it. I bashed through them and they clicked shut behind me. Then a breeze was blowing fresh and clean on my face and leaves crunched underfoot. I was out of the tunnel and in some kind of forest.

It was all totally strange and scary, but I had a funny feeling this was more than just a weird video dream. It was getting horribly real and I jumped as something touched my face. It was only a trailing green vine with little black berries on it. I tried one and it tasted like apricot, so I knew at least I wouldn't starve while I was trapped in this video underworld.

The sun was very hot and I could hardly see through the trees. They were crazy trees, too, some wrinkled and bent like bad-tempered old people, some smooth with big upward-spreading branches. Some even had two sets of leaves, thick and broad or thin and spoon-shaped. The berry vines threaded through everything. There were many flowers; little dots of red, big petals of yellow with blue dots, even thick purple, orange and green clusters together. Green vines ran everywhere like a network and everything was peaceful and quiet. I knew I was safe, because everyone knows that vampires can't stand the sunlight.

I should have been more scared, but it was as though something inside me was saying this was all OK. I looked behind to see what I'd come out of. It was a huge round metal cave like a monster exhaust pipe with a massive tall metal fin towering over it, tangled with vines to the tip. It looked like part of a giant jet aircraft, but that was impossible. There was a rustling noise beside me and something like a flying cat leaped from one branch to another. It wasn't a cat, but a monkey with arms like a hangglider and a cat's head. It hissed at me, hung by one paw for a moment and then disappeared.

A bird came down. It was sparrow-sized, but bright yellow with a red crest. It hovered over my shoulder then flew off. I was really puzzled now because none of this belonged, even in a super-real video game, and a strange unlocking feeling in my body was saying this *was* real. Then something else rustled by and caught in the vines. I turned again, but it wasn't an animal this time.

It was a spear.

Suddenly, ten metres ahead, something crashed into sight. It was big and broad-shouldered with an armour-plated skin and snarling face like a sawn-off crocodile snout. It was dull olive-green all over, and growled something in a gobbly voice I didn't understand. Then another two-legged crocodile-thing crashed into sight, holding a crossbow, and the first one pointed at me. 'Kill,' it said.

I understood that all right! The second creature was already aiming and I ducked as the bolt whizzed overhead. They were charging towards me and I knew I had to get away. But I was glued to the ground, unable to move, when ahead, a pair of legs in the same silver-grey overalls I was wearing, appeared out of a tree as someone swung down. It was a brown-skinned girl with dark blonde and red hair, and she turned to face me. Her silver-grey track suit had the name YOONA black-lettered over the pocket.

'Back to the ship!' she shouted.

Ship? She shoved me and I just tripped and fell. The crocodile-monsters were pounding towards us, the second one reloading its crossbow. Yoona stood there facing them, and put a long tube like a flute to her lips, whistling sharply in very high notes. The first monster stopped so quickly that the second one banged into it. Yoona blew again and they pressed four-clawed paws over little ear-slits in the side of their heads. She played another strong note.

'Go on, you silly kloppers, move!' she called out.

The one holding the reloaded crossbow dropped it and ran. The first one stood snarling for a moment. He had on a leather strap-harness and big shells on his shoulders like armour-plate. Then he turned to walk away. Yoona lowered the flute, but I was still watching because I knew what I'd do if I were him. And he did that – he ducked to grab the crossbow and turned to fire.

Yoona was waiting for that, too. She jammed the flute to her lips and blew a loud sweet blast. The leader yelled with pain and the crossbow bolt shot off up into the trees. He dropped the weapon and turned, crashing back after the other one like a runaway tank. Yoona grabbed my arm.

'Come on. They're too thick to know when to stop.'

She was pulling me back to the metal cave, but I held back. Yoona understood, pointing to her black-lettered name and said, 'I'm sorry. My name is Yoona. Explanations back in Deepwater, Conn.'

Conn? And the word, Deepwater? But the crashing sounds came back with high clicking shouts, so I let her pull me along and we went back down the round metal cave, through those locking doors. 'What is this?' I yelled, finding my voice for the first time.

'Exhaust system of the ship,' said Yoona.

That really knocked me! If this was an exhaust system, like the exhaust-pipe of a car, then how big was the whole ship? We stopped at the last door and Yoona pointed at a trap-door and ladder overhead. 'Up and over,' she said.

'Why not straight ahead?' I asked.

'We can't . . .' She broke off, looking at me very startled. 'Which way did you come?'

'Through there,' I said, pointing through the last door into that winding corridor.

Yoona just looked at me and then went through. A solid light-bar shone down on us and later I learned this was one of Deepwater's defence systems against alien invaders. We went back down that winding corridor to the next room and Yoona knelt to press her hand on the black water-bed floor. 'COL is getting stronger,' she said. 'A week ago, we couldn't walk on this.'

'What's COL?' I asked. The super-knowing feeling was still running through me, though.

'COL is a bio-computer and this is a forcefield. COL is sealing it off. That's good, as it will be able to take orders soon.' She grinned at me. 'Come on.'

We were back through that open, massive crystal door into the huge football-field room where I had woken up. I looked at the three closed caskets, but Yoona pulled me on. We went through that high-ceilinged room and through the second door into a corridor stretching about half a kilometre in length. I was starting to think that Deepwater had no end. Lights came on over us and shut off as we passed, flickering overhead like night and day. Yoona must have sensed my puzzlement, because she smiled again. 'You'll understand better up top,' she said.

Up top? Now we were through the corridor into a long room with narrow beds on either side. On one of them lay a girl of another colour, blue-skinned, blue-haired, with the name LIS black-lettered on her silver-grey tunic. She slept as though really zonked, like Mum after a hard day in the shop.

At the end of the room, a flight of steps led upwards. Yoona pulled me up them, into another room, one that made everything spin like a giddy mad dream. I saw a long floor, consoles and eye-shaped windows looking into forest. In two of the black chairs were a boy with brown-red skin and a green-skinned girl with long green hair, whispering to each other and turning to look at us. The girl had a black eye-patch and a closed cross look on her face. My dream was still strange, but getting very real.

'This is Conn,' said Yoona. 'He's from the eighth casket.'

The brown-red boy and the green girl just looked at me as though I was from another planet. I thought *they* were. 'You're red,' I heard myself saying. 'And green.' The girl was black-lettered GRET.

'Had a look at *yourself*?' said the boy. His black-lettered name was BREN.

I didn't answer because I was looking at myself and saw what he meant. The consoles behind those black chairs were blank and I could see my reflection clearly. I was looking at my own face, but with brown-red skin like Bren's, my hair cut short and ending in a neat long dreadlock. Yoona grabbed my arm and pointed up another flight of steps. 'Up top,' she said, 'then you'll understand.'

The spiral staircase led straight up and a weird dream-like feeling came over me as I followed Yoona up and out, it seemed, on to the top of the world.

It was like standing on the roof of a multi-storey building. All round were scattered green patches as though someone had picked up handfuls of trees and thrown them like confetti. They spread out thickly round us, then became smaller clumps and even single trees. Between them were fields in different green colours, some yellow and red with flowers, and streams sparkled a bright sunlit blue between them. We were standing beside a long twin-barrelled gun and around, in a big circle, were cracked pieces of glass like a huge, half-broken egg.

'The bubble-turret of our laser cannon,' said Yoona. 'It was smashed when we crash-landed.'

Ahead, Deepwater rounded off to a snout and below, along the sides, sharp wide fins stuck out, curled with green vines. Behind, stretching out like the massive silver-plate back of a monster whale, the top ended in that high tail-fin,

9

and I knew what this thing was – as though it came on-screen in my mind, like data off the school computer.

Deepwater was a crashed spaceship.

'I know it's too much to take in at once,' said Yoona. She paused. 'It was for Robbie and Denie.'

Robbie and Denie. I knew those names. I turned to her and Yoona looked at me, the wind streaming out her long, thick hair. 'What about Robbie and Denie?' I said. 'Are they on this spaceship too?'

'So you did know them, Conn?' It was strange, the way Yoona said this, as though she knew the answers but was afraid to ask.

'Yes, I know them. From school.'

There was something slow and careful in the way Yoona spoke that suddenly made me afraid. I knew her tone of voice, the same as a cop had had on that night he knocked at our door and told us about the accident – my dad dead after a singing gig in Australia. Yoona went on in that same careful, quiet voice and everything was spinning crazily round her words.

'Robbie and Denie are dead.'

2 Not being Meatgrinder

Robbie and Denie are dead. Robbie and Denie are dead. The words echoed round me and Yoona's face seemed to blur and go dark, and I heard her say something about prexing. I opened my eyes again and was lying back in the storm-drain.

I sat up. What a crazy dream! Maybe burned sausages and melted ice-cream sort of affected the brain, I thought, and blinked. But it was funny because when you wake up, you *know* it was a dream – but this one still somehow seemed real. And Denie Miles being dead . . . the same Denie who yesterday shouted something . . . I had Mum, Roger and the cops to think about, but suddenly seeing Denie was the most important thing of all.

I looked round but there was nobody in sight except a woman jogging and she looked too short for an undercover cop. I got on my bike and pedalled out, keeping a careful eye open. It was lucky I did, because I saw Reeboks coming and just had time to hide before he went past.

His name is Graeme Wilson, but he's called Reeboks because of his classy footwear. He was leaning over the handlebars of his bike, his glasses glinting in the sun, skinny as a hungry ferret and on his way to the storm-drain, I was sure. Well, he wouldn't find me there and that sudden feeling in my stomach pushed me on to find Denie.

She was at the school hockey game. She's good mates with Robbie Mikkelson now and was watching him play. She was reading one of her astronomy books, too, because

Denie has a thing about wanting to go to outer space. It was creepy seeing her after the Yoona dream-girl had talked about her, but I went up and kneeled beside her.

'Who's Chibbi?' I said.

She jumped. Maybe I was a bit close. 'Meatgrinder?' she said, then quickly changed it. 'Connal? Who did you say?' Denie has a nice face, a bit freckled and round with short brown hair. 'Who?'

'Chibbi. Once you said to talk to her if I had funny dreams.'

'Did I?' Denie looked puzzled, then her face changed again, as though she remembered something she couldn't find words for. Then she rattled, 'Chibbi Orduna, graduate student, finishing her genetic project at the university lab this weekend,' firing the words off like machine-gun bullets. She blinked again, as though puzzled, as the end-of-game whistle blew and the players came off the field.

'Thanks,' I said, and was about to get on my bike when Robbie came up. He threw down his hockey stick, grinned at Denie and then saw me.

'What're you doing here, Meatgrinder?'

'Just asking about the university,' said Denie quickly.

Robbie grinned. 'He wouldn't know what a university was.'

Just yesterday, I would have replied, 'I know what a smack in the mouth is,' and maybe shown it. But not today. I looked at them and like a horrible echo from darkness, came Yoona's voice. Robbie and Denie are dead . . . are dead . . . dead. Then Denie's voice, sharp with fear, came through the darkness.

'Connal, what're you looking at us like that for?'

'Nothing,' I said. 'Sorry.'

I couldn't look at them any more. I got on my bike and cycled off, but when I looked back they were there, as though frozen against the background. Then another bike squealed its brakes ahead of mine and a high voice shouted:

'Hey, Meatgrinder!'

It was Reeboks – no, Graeme, I had to call him now – and he looked back to Robbie and Denie. 'What're you talking to them for? They're the enemy.'

Maybe even a few hours ago, I would have nodded. But now, I didn't know. 'I've got to go somewhere, Graeme.'

'Reeboks, I'm Reeboks, not Graeme,' he said, and as my bike moved off, he yelled, 'Hey, we've got things to talk about—'

Maybe we did, but right then I wasn't listening. 'See you later,' I said.

'Where're you going?' he shouted. 'Denie? Meatgrinder, she's a trouble-maker, she tried to bust us up.'

Yes, and you helped by not being straight with me, I thought, putting on speed to lose him. Two sharp corners, a short-cut, a speed-boost and Reeboks was lost. I forgot about him and went even more quickly. I knew where the university was and although it was Friday evening, there were still lots of people around. None of them looked like a Chibbi, so I kept circling until I was round the back and found a young woman sorting through a stack of cartons.

'Hi,' I said uncertainly. 'Chibbi?'

'If you're the mini-van, you're too early,' she said without turning round.

'No, I've been prexing,' I said.

I should have found a more roundabout way to tell her. She straightened a bit too quickly and the stack of boxes fell, one hitting her on the head. She turned round slowly, rubbing her head, and the first thing I saw was a great pair of brown eyes and a nice wide smile, smiling a bit puzzled.

'You're what . . . ?' she said.

'Yoona mentioned prexing,' I said, 'so did Denie. She said you'd know about it, I don't.' She just looked at me, maybe a bit dazed because the carton had hit her, so I went on. 'My name's Meatgrind – Connal.'

'Meatgrind-Connal, that's an interesting name.' A grin

took shape on her wide mouth and she motioned me inside. 'Shall we talk about this?'

I followed her into a room with a long table, glass tubes and all sorts of hi-tech gear. Chibbi was about twenty, wearing black jeans, a long blue shirt scrambled with all sorts of colours and a yellow headband round her black curls. She looked at me, frowned a little until her face cleared then she pointed a finger. 'Got you. The boy who started a fight at my lecture.' She was right, I had started a fight with Robbie, a few days before all this happened. She went on, 'You booted that other boy, Robbie.' Yes I had, but now a young woman, a hundred-million dream-years away, had told me Robbie was dead—

'Denie said you'd know about prexing,' I burst out. I *had* to tell someone.

Chibbi just looked at me and her smile went serious. She went over to a table cluttered with stuff and said, 'I've only got coffee. OK with you?'

'Sure.' I didn't like coffee but being on the run from the cops meant I had to get used to anything. I sat down on a stool and she whistled as she made the coffee, glancing back at me.

'Three spoons of sugar?' she said, grinning again.

'How did you know?' I said.

'Oh, you look like a three-sugar guy.' Chibbi sipped her coffee and put it down. Her brown eyes went sharp, seeing right through me, her soft voice also going sharp. 'Now tell me about your prexing.'

'Nothing,' I said.

Chibbi just nodded and let me talk. I told her everything, from talking to Denie and waking up on the Deepwater spaceship, the kloppers – everything. She sipped her coffee as she listened and never once took her eyes from me. Then she sat silent and I started to get a bit mad. Parents and teachers always sit like that when they don't believe you or want to put me down. So I jumped up. I was scared anyway

14

with the cops looking for me, so I yelled really loud. 'I don't care if you believe me or not!'

'So who says I don't?' Chibbi's voice went as sharp as her brown eyes, so sharp that I shut my mouth and even forgot to frown. 'Now do you want to hear what I know?' she said.

Yes, I did. So Chibbi told me what she knew. Denie Miles had come to her with the same story about being on a Deepwater spaceship that went round the universe and crash-landed on Earth. She had told her that being on Deepwater and then back on Earth was called prexing, pre-existing. The crew of Deepwater were cloned from gene cells for the super-long voyage and those gene cells – from today – had an echo of today's memory, of the person the gene was taken from. So a kid cloned from that gene could have two lives.

I didn't understand it and Chibbi admitted she wasn't sure either. '*But—* ' she said, 'I do believe this is more than three kids with crazy dreams. I'm here for a day or so and I'll give you my address and phone number. You tell me what happens – OK, Connal?'

'OK,' I replied. It was nice hearing her call me Connal and I nearly told her about the cops chasing me, but didn't. I never trust adults the first time I meet them. As I got up to go, she put a hand on my arm.

'You be careful, Connal,' she said.

There was something in the way she said it that made me a bit scared. But Torkan the Awesome never showed fear, so I couldn't. I just nodded. For just a moment, I wanted to turn round and scream everything out, but Roger had said that only stupid kids put all their cards on the table at once.

'OK,' I said again.

Chibbi sat with her legs crossed, her coffee cup at her lips and her brown eyes looking over it at me. In that moment I was suddenly back across time and space in a black bright-sparkling unknown.

I was on the road home before realising I couldn't go there until the heat was off. So I bought a hamburger and fries and headed back to the storm-drain. I swung out wide, though, to pass near Mum's shop and see how many cop cars were parked outside. There were none, but I didn't dare enter in case they were waiting inside. It was a good little place – Mum had worked really hard getting it and I wanted to go back more than anything. But I had to stay in the storm-drain, together with that incredible sharp dream still in my head. So I headed back and the first thing I saw was Reeboks cruising round. I yelled, really mad, 'Graeme, stop biking round. Anybody can see I'm in the drain!'

He pushed his bike under cover and came over, swinging a bag. Normally I have to look for Reeboks, but today he was all over me. The bag had chips, tins of baked beans and soft drinks, even the newspaper. The headline was 'Ramraider arrested', and in smaller words below, ' . . . Proceeds still missing.'

'Proceeds' meant all the jewels, watches and rings crammed into Roger's bag. Graeme glinted his glasses intently at me, leaning over the handlebars like a homing missile on target. 'Meatgrinder, do you need any help?'

'Not Meatgrinder – Connal,' I muttered, feeling something wash over me like slimy water.

'Hey, are you OK?' Reeboks asked.

No, I wasn't OK. I'd been on a crashed spaceship and it was still too real to think of it as a dream-state; and a dream-girl had told me that two kids I knew were dead. And the cops were after me.

'I gotta go.' Reeboks was still giving me curious looks. 'I'll tell Mum you're spending the night with me, OK?'

'Thanks, Reeboks,' I said, forgetting to use his proper name. Then for a moment he seemed to go flat as a paper image, as though he didn't really exist. 'Yes, Ree – Graeme—' I said, the words slashing like black water on my tongue. My voice echoed and from a long way in the

16

blackness, Graeme was asking again if I was OK. Then his voice and everything spun tightly and someone else was talking to me. I opened my eyes on Deepwater and Yoona was sitting over me.

'Are you OK?' she said.

Now I knew all this was *not* a dream.

3   The blood place

I was back in the control room of the spaceship. The green girl with the black eye-patch was there and the blue girl I'd seen asleep, LIS black-lettered on her tunic. Gret ignored me, intent on her console, but Lis came over with a big grin and stuck out her hand.

'Hi. I'm Lis. The first prex is always scary.'

Yoona gave me some water and a small fruit like a plum. I wanted to ask about Robbie and Denie, but decided to wait; they'd tell me when they were ready. Gret pressed a crystal point and a big overhead screen sprang into life. It was a view of the side of the ship. The two-legged crocodile-things were holding a tree-trunk, yellow sap still running from its fresh-cut end, and using it like a ram against the port.

'What are they?'

'Reptile-humanoids,' said Yoona. 'Martian species, they are called "swampies" or "kloppers".'

'What are they doing here on Earth?'

'Must have been part of the gene drop,' said Yoona, but she shrugged uncertainly.

'Why don't you go out and ask them?' muttered Gret.

Lis nudged her with another grin. 'Stop being such a sour-puss, Gret.' She grinned at me. 'Gret doesn't like prexing Earthkids.'

'Keep an eye on the kloppers,' said Yoona, and took my arm. 'Come on, I'll show you something.'

We went below. The boy Bren was on one of the beds,

asleep. We went through the door and down that long corridor she had brought me up. The lighting flickered on as we did, showing the long corridor stretching ahead. 'You must have a lot of questions,' said Yoona, walking quickly.

'Why the different colours. Green, blue and red?' It was the first one that escaped all the others crowding on my tongue.

'Genetic tinting,' said Yoona. 'The first Martian colonists were genetically made and tinted different colours to stop them returning to Earth – to keep them separate.'

'People wouldn't do that,' I said.

'Would people pollute their planet to death?' replied Yoona with a bitter smile. She stopped at the door to the NUN chamber and put her hand, palm first, on a symbol in the centre. It clicked open and we went inside.

I've already said how big the NUN chamber was. But what really got to me was the silence and that creepy sensation of being in something that was once living – much as a bio-computer could live. And now it held the bodies of three Deepwater crew, two of them kids I'd talked with at a game of hockey, just a time-blink ago, across the prex blackness.

Yoona stopped at the closed caskets. She didn't have to bring me down here, but she wanted to because it made her story more real. The NUN chamber was the heart of Deepwater, the monster-terminal where they were cloned from gene cells and where NUN tried to keep them as children. The closed caskets were made out of Martian rain-crystal; inside those boxes of alien glass were the bodies of Robbie and Denie, and Zak, who fired NUN's shot of self-destruction.

'You have to understand everything, Conn,' said Yoona softly.

I wanted to. But all this was so awesome. And I knew I was changing. I was thinking things, using words and thoughts in a way I never had before. I had come out of one of those rain-crystal caskets and now Yoona looked at me across them and told me what had happened since Deepwater crash-landed back on Earth at the end of what was its second journey round the universe.

At the end of the second mission, Yoona and the others thought it was over. They had to find a means of regenerating the human race from the gene bank they had saved. They believed that COL would guide them and a way would be found when Deepwater had recharged. So they put themselves into deep-sleep for six months, but when they woke up Deepwater was still recharging. The food and water machines were not producing, so they went out into the newly grown forests of Earth. In just six months, the gene drop returned fully-grown life to the planet. But when they went out to get food and water, the kloppers were waiting.

That was when Robbie – on Deepwater, they called him Reb – and Denie – known as Cei – were hit. The kloppers came out of nowhere. Robbie was struck by a crossbow bolt and they got Denie as she tried to save him. So like Zak before, Yoona and the others put them back in the caskets; to hope that one day, somehow, they might come back to life. But I could sense, in the way Yoona said those last words, that she knew there was no hope. NUN was the life-giver, but they had destroyed NUN to save themselves; so there was no hope at all.

Yoona was standing by Robbie's casket. She didn't say so, but I knew from the way she touched it and the catch in her voice when she spoke his name. She stood there, strong and proud, telling me things that must have cut her up inside, being the commander she was. She was in charge of Deepwater, in charge of the human gene bank, and she would fight to the last to save it.

Then she sighed and the noise picked up in the echoes, like a lost wind blowing. I looked up and just for a second, something looked down like a huge eye blinking awake. Yoona passed her hand softly over the rain-crystal surface of the casket and whispered a word I could not hear. Then she smiled, a strong smile, but she was still being cut up inside.

'You rest now. Gret and I are going out to get food and water.' She didn't say it, but I knew what they had given me was their last.

'I want to go,' I said, knowing I growled because I was trying not to think about Denie and Robbie. 'I want to be useful.'

'Stay here and rest,' said Yoona.

'I've got to go,' I growled again, and I think I even yelled a bit because the echoes went up like a wave round us. 'I want to be useful!'

Yoona looked at me and some of the sparkling light from the rain-crystal seemed to reflect on her face as she smiled.

'That's just about what Robbie and Denie would say,' she said and without looking back led the way back over to the distant door. Her footsteps caught the silence and again, just for a second, I sensed that eye-blink high above like something waking up. Then I followed the echo of Yoona's footsteps and tried not to think about leaving Robbie and Denie behind me in this big strange place.

We found Bren and Gret sitting on a bed together. They stood up, exchanged looks, as we came in. I knew a power-play when I saw it. They were pushing Yoona because she was in command and they didn't like it.

'We need food,' said Bren, scowling. 'Let's get out now while they're at the other end.'

'Yes,' said Gret. 'Now.'

Yoona looked from one to the other. She frowned, but nodded. 'All right, but be careful.'

Bren slammed his hand over a button, opening a door at the other end of the lower deck. It was one of four doors leading to a bigger port and I followed through, feeling a little alarm tingle in my body. 'How do you know they're just at the exhaust?'

'Because they're stupid,' said Gret. I didn't like her tone either.

Bren paused, his hand on the release button for the last port. 'Don't worry, Earthkid, you're not in danger.'

I'd already made up my mind to fight this guy; and sensed the tone in Gret's voice. Like some kids at school, it meant 'thicko' and 'zero' – it meant nothing I said mattered. 'Maybe they're not so silly,' I said. 'Maybe they're making a noise that end and keeping quiet here.'

'And maybe you're just a prexing Earthkid,' growled Bren as he hit the last button and the door slid open.

I pushed him hard and he crashed over. The spear zoomed over us both, and beside me Yoona ducked, slamming the button again as crossbow bolts whizzed through; the bushes were parting and the two-legged olive-green tanks came charging through. The door shut and more bolts clinked against it.

One of the bolts had cut Bren's arm. He put a hand to it and I think his brown-red face went a bit pale at seeing his own red blood. 'You were right,' he said, and put out his hand. It was smeared with his blood, but I took it and Bren grinned a little. 'Maybe you can teach us a thing or two.'

'We did respect Reb and Cei,' said Gret softly, her face still set in a pale green scowl, but I keyed to the word 'respect'. OK, these kids weren't friends, but they did hang together; Robbie and Denie had been in good company.

There was more blood coming between the fingers Bren kept clenched over his arm as we went back to the lower deck. Gret began bandaging it and Yoona kicked up a trap-door in the deck. 'There's another way out,' she said. 'Come on, Conn.'

'I'll go!' snapped Gret.

'I need you here,' said Yoona calmly.

Gret was really annoyed. She flashed her green eyes and didn't look at me; it was the insult that mattered. Yoona just stood quiet and all Gret's rage-snapping crashed like storm waves against a concrete wall. Gret was always pushing, but I think she also hated being left out. She still scowled as Yoona showed me the way below.

The other way out of Deepwater was underneath. Down a flight of steps nearly as long as the NUN corridor to a bottom deck, holding a big spacecraft that Yoona called a Wingfish. Once there were two of them, but the other had gone fighting a monster off Jupiter. Yoona led me to a stair bay below the Wingfish, where the iron-glass window was blotted out with thick, deep-brown earth.

'Deepwater's buried to the nose,' she said softly. 'But maybe we can dig out the loose soil – the kloppers won't be watching somewhere buried.'

'OK,' I grinned.

It was easier than we thought. The soil and undergrowth only just covered the bottom port and the full, rich bird-twitter and strong smell of a living planet hit us as we went out into yellow-hot sunlight, the airlock-port sliding shut behind us.

Yoona stood there for a moment, looking round. 'Wonderful,' she breathed, as though in a magic land. She pointed up at the sun through the trees.

'The sun?' I nodded. 'Sure, it's OK.'

Yoona smiled at me and began walking. It took me a moment to work out that she was a space-woman who had spent most of her life in a long enclosed spaceship; the sun really was magic. She smiled again and started walking into the forest, laser rifle held across her body.

'I thought you'd seen a lot of sun, you've such a great tan,' I said. Her skin was as brown as mine.

'The same genetic tinting,' replied Yoona. 'Everyone on Earth got it when the ozone layer went and radiation became too strong. My dad moved to South Mars and met my mum there.' She looked at me. 'That was when Earth was nearly dead.'

24

'We never knew the pollution was so bad,' I said, a leaf touching my face and a little blue-black insect ducking across my eye. Then I realised that was wrong. 'Yes, we knew. We just didn't do anything.'

Yoona nodded, a lot of shadow falling over her face as she pressed up to a tree. She smiled, her mouth full of shadow as she made to speak. Then there was a little snap-clicking sound and Yoona pulled me to the tree after her.

Ahead, two kloppers had appeared. It was my first close look and they were impressive, about two metres tall with thick shoulders and a heavily-scaled body like armour-plate. Their heads were pointed, their eyes narrow and slitted, and they looked mean and ugly. Both held those powerful crossbows.

They paused in the clearing, sunlight-shadow making a pattern on their scaly bodies, turning their thick-snouted heads from side to side, then kept going.

'Just a patrol,' whispered Yoona.

She pulled me further into cover. Something chattered overhead and a little bird with zigzag-patterned green and red feathers fluttered into view, squeaked at us and ducked out of sight. Yoona pulled me even further and thick green creepers tangled round us. 'They don't like thick cover. Slows them down,' she said. 'Come on.'

She began pulling some big round purple berries off a tree. I tasted one. 'What are these?' I said.

'We don't know any of the fruit,' said Yoona. She moved on and pulled off some yellow cone-shaped things. 'They're new, like everything else.' She looked back at me. 'Lend a hand, Conn.'

I started to pull the fruit off, but looked round. 'Shouldn't one of us be on guard?' I asked.

'They don't know we're here.'

I think it was lucky for Yoona and the others that I woke up from the casket when I did. They'd been on their own too long and, like the clever kids at school, thought they knew it all. They didn't, though, and Yoona knew *that* when a crossbow bolt split the yellow cone she was about to reach for. Yoona grabbed for the flute in her belt, but another bolt smashed it from her hand.

There were three of them, crashing through the undergrowth at us. I remember thinking it strange the third one didn't fire, but then it did and the bolt went into the tree beside my head. Yoona grabbed my arm, yelling at me to run, and we somehow stamped through the creepers. The kloppers followed and managed to get themselves tangled. But they were still between us and Deepwater.

Yoona grabbed my hand. 'Listen!' she whispered. A series of loud clicking shouts rang out behind us and were answered in the distance. 'That's them, calling the others.'

We kept running to the front and as we did, more kloppers appeared at the side, with more clicking shouts as they saw us. Now bolts were whizzing from the side as well as from behind. 'At least they're bad shots,' panted Yoona as we took a flying leap over some thick fork-leaved bushes, into a gully.

'Are they?' I grabbed her arm, even then thinking it was strange they were always such bad shots. 'In here!'

A tree had fallen over the gully, the uprooted stump tearing a hole, and we collapsed in there together. Next moment there was a loud thud and a pair of scaled olive-green klopper legs appeared in front of us. The heavy four-clawed feet had leather sandals and cross-straps on the legs. Another pair of klopper feet appeared and both scrambled up the far bank. But there were more clicking shouts from behind and the whistle of another bolt passing overhead.

'They're either really bad shots or not aiming at us,' I whispered. Yoona looked at me with surprise and shock. She was breathing quickly and we both stayed silent until the footsteps had died away. 'Just because they look solid and thick, doesn't mean they're stupid,' I said.

'Conn, what do you mean, not aiming at us?' We pressed back as another pair of the green-scaled legs lumbered past.

'Maybe they were driving us somewhere.' I don't know why I said that, it just static-buzzed under my tongue.

'Let's see, then. We're behind them now.'

I could see why Yoona was commander. She thought fast and was afraid of nothing. I followed as she skipped ahead in her long-legged way, through the cover. Then she slowed down. There was no sound round us except the frightened chatter of birds and, once, the distant clicking shout of a klopper. A bright little pink-feathered bird with orange and yellow spots looked at us before flapping away. A dark red, furry, four-legged thing crashed into the undergrowth. I stopped, noticing something.

'Hey. There's no bird-noise any more.'

Yoona looked round, listening, and nodded. Bird sounds had always been there, like the different notes of trickling water, but now they were silent. One of those little cat-monkeys appeared in the trees, saw us and shot off.

'When we first came out of Deepwater, they would sit on our heads,' said Yoona quietly. 'Now they're scared of us.'

A little further on, we saw why. The bush cleared and dipped into a little grassy valley. Grass is green, but this grass was coloured an ugly, sticky brown-red and was sprinkled with a strange fluttering weed. The weed was feathers, scattered all over and glued to the ground by dark, hard patches of blood. Between them were birds and animals, stripped of their flesh, bodies torn apart and with blowflies humming over them. It was like a slaughterhouse and I knew two things at once. Kloppers were flesh-eaters and this was where they cut up their food.

No wonder the birds and animals were afraid of us.

Yoona put her face down into the green grass we were still on, her lips tight together and her eyes shut. I knew she was trying hard not to be sick and suddenly I felt the same way; I used to like all those Hollywood movies where people got ripped up by bullets and the hero always tore his enemies apart, but this was real and the smell was awful. I put my face down, too, and took a deep breath of fresh grass, letting it brush my cheeks. I wanted to breathe in the sweetness of things living.

Yoona raised her head again, her face very pale under her brown skin. She breathed out hard and shook her head so that her hair went round her face. 'I suppose you're more used to that,' she said. 'Your society chopped up animals for food, didn't they?'

'Yes,' I said, but it sounded horrible the way she said it, as though we were just like the kloppers.

'Let's get out of here, Conn.'

I nodded. With the kloppers still around, it was dangerous to stay in one place too long. We went on a way, then stopped in the shelter of a thick bronze-leaved bush covered with little green and white flowers. They had a nice sharp smell and Yoona put one in the collar of her track suit. I still had a crossbow bolt stuck in my belt and she pulled it out, looking at it.

'Kloppers didn't have weapons on Mars. They were too primitive.'

'They've got them now,' I said. 'And gear. Maybe they got smarter.' Then without my knowing why, another thought came into my mind. 'Maybe somebody taught them.'

Yoona looked at me, her eyes wide. She opened her mouth to ask a question, putting the bolt on the grass as she did. A spear plunged down where her hand had been. A line of kloppers was storming towards us and Yoona grabbed my arm. 'Come on!'

As we began to run, there was a sudden howling and screaming round us as though the earth itself was screaming at that horrible blood-place. Even with the kloppers behind us, Yoona stopped for a moment.

28

'That's Deepwater!' she yelled.

A crossbow bolt stuck in the ground between us and I yelled back. 'Move!'

We kept running, but ahead, through the trees, other kloppers were running. More bolts and spears whizzed by and the howling went on. The ground shook like in an earthquake as we headed for more trees. Ahead, more of the olive-green tank-bodies recoiled as something coloured burst among them. Two more little silver sticks flashed in the sunlight as they tumbled down and exploded into more smoke. Now some of the kloppers were shooting into the air and Yoona yelled, grabbed my arm and pointing up. Through the different-coloured drifting smoke came the strangest creature I'd ever seen on this new Earth-planet.

It was long and a shiny blue-silver, with bulging insect eyes and an upturned tail like a scorpion, and it was skimming fast towards us like some fantastic monster flying insect. Then one bug-eye snapped open and I saw Gret stand up, her green hair flying in the wind. The other bug-eye opened for Lis, who chucked down another silver stick that burst in a cloud of fizzing green smoke.

Bolts were clanging up against our hull and I knew the kloppers were close. Gret was bringing the little machine down and Lis reached out to grab Yoona and pull her in. I glanced behind; a line of armoured kloppers were bursting through the smoke.

'Up!' I yelled and threw myself over the bank, clinging to the opened cockpit cover. Gret took the thing sharply up into the air, followed by the usual badly-aimed volley of bolts and spears, then in such a sharp circle that I was nearly thrown off. Yoona grabbed me and we set off at tree-top level towards Deepwater and that strange inhuman howling sound. A last bolt flew past before the kloppers were lost from sight.

I found out later that this thing was called an OMA,

Outside Maintenance Auxiliary for repairs in deep space.

'How did you get it working?' shouted Yoona, her hand still tight on mine.

'All the systems came on-line,' Gret yelled back, 'right when that siren noise did.'

We were going down fast, into the trees and flying straight for the hulk of Deepwater. A circular side-port was opening and we flew right in. The OMA grew legs, dropping neatly on to the deck as the porthole slid shut behind us.

I thought the howling noise would have stopped, too, but it was even louder, coming from *inside* Deepwater. We ran through the airlocks to the lower deck, then the upper deck. Bren was at the controls and Yoona ran over. 'Have we got voice-ac with COL?' she shouted.

'No,' yelled Bren back over the noise, 'but all the systems are back on-line like—' and he hesitated.

Yoona looked at him. 'Pre-programming. Deepwater's done that before.'

'Yoona!' Lis was yelling from the spiral staircase and the shattered bubble-turret. Yoona ran up the stairs and I followed. Lis was on top, holding the gun-chair in one hand as she pointed.

Below, the ground and trees were shaking and quivering. For a moment I glimpsed olive-green forms running alongside Deepwater until they disappeared as the spaceship bucked beneath us. Lis yelled again and hung on to the gun-chair. I skidded forward and ended up against one of the large glass broken walls. Now Deepwater was shaking along its length and bits of creeper were tossed up as it shuddered like a beached whale, raising itself on rocket-flippers.

Yoona pushed me to the hatch and yelled for Lis to follow. We tumbled down the spiral staircase and the ship gave an extra heave as Yoona slammed the hatch. Suddenly the howling stopped and for a moment Deepwater was silent.

Then a new power surge started. This one did not shake

and jerk, but seemed to flex the ship like a huge muscle; it hummed and vibrated and burst a bright yellow-and-black static electricity through Deepwater, flashing round Bren and throwing him back from the consoles. Through the iron-glass windows, the ground seemed to change and the control deck steepened. All of us knew then what was happening, but as it did, a funny spinning blackness came over me and through it came Yoona's scared and tense words.

'Deepwater is taking off!'

4 Ramraider Roger returns

I opened my eyes and a hand still held mine tightly.

'Yoona?' I muttered.

'Who's Yoona?'

I opened my eyes. Graeme/Reeboks was there, his eyes darting all round the storm-drain. My watch said about four o'clock and I shook my head, feeling giddy and sick. Reeboks opened a can of juice and gave it to me. 'Did you sleep here last night?' he said.

I nodded. I couldn't remember sleeping here, but my body did, from the aches and pains. 'I brought some food and stuff,' he said.

He was still looking round and lifted open my own bag. 'What're you looking for?' I said.

'Nothing,' said Reeboks, smiling brightly. 'Listen, the cops are looking for you.'

'Cops!' I shouldn't have jumped, but I did. 'Did you cover for me?'

Reeboks hesitated. 'I can't really, Meat – Connal. You see—'

'You said you would!'

'No, no, listen,' Reeboks yelled. 'I would truly, but my dad's a bank manager and his bank's joined with another one, so he's even more important now—'

'Reeboks, I don't care if your dad owns a *million* banks—'

'You will if you lose your mortgage,' he interrupted.

I was about to yell myself, but stopped and put the can

down. Our mortgage is with the same bank as Reebok's dad, and Mum had to work really hard to get it, being a solo parent and all that. And it costs a lot to keep it going. Reeboks says that knowing him helps, because he puts in a good word with his dad. He went on, still looking round, and put some gum in his mouth. 'Banks chop a mortgage if there's any trouble and the cops would tell them – tell Dad.' He looked at me, chewing gum quickly. 'Better hurry before they come.'

That was it. I couldn't let Mum lose the shop. 'Thanks, Graeme,' I said.

'Hey, I'm Reeboks, remember.'

'Denie said nicknames were silly.'

'Stuff her, I like it. Reeboks are classy.'

He had to shout this last bit because I was outside the drain, pulling my bike out of cover and heading for the road. Reeboks cycled beside me, still talking; sometimes he never stops. 'Hey, Connal, do you know anything about the gear Roger stole? I hope it's nowhere round the house. 'Cos then you and your mum will be in real trouble.'

'What d'you mean?' I shouted back. Sometimes Graeme Wilson gets very close to a smack in the mouth.

'You'll be accessories,' he shouted, making us sound like something out of a fancy dress shop. 'If they get the loot, your mum will end up in court. So don't tell the cops anything.'

I braked so hard that Reeboks went five metres ahead and swallowed his gum. He came biking back up, unwrapping another packet.

'Are you sure?'

Reeboks nodded up and down several times, his jaw moving fast again. 'Sure I'm sure. Dad knows these things.' Then he said suddenly, 'Connal, if you do know where the gear is, don't tell anyone.' I looked at him, remembering how he nosed around the storm-drain, but there was a really innocent look on his face and he said quickly, 'Don't tell

34

anyone and they can't do anything.'

We cycled up to the top of my road and I stopped again because someone else on a bike was waiting there. It was Denie Miles. Her face as pale in the twilight and there was a tense look on her face. 'I've been waiting to talk to you, Connal. You seemed really spaced out this morning. Is anything wrong?'

Yoona, the new Earth, the Deepwater spaceship, it was all exploding back into my mind, even how the spaceship bucked as it took off. It was a crazy dream, but so was all this, two crazy dreams colliding with each other. 'Spaced out,' Denie had said – I was spaced out across maybe half a million years. I heard myself answering her, speaking in a low voice as though nobody else existed.

'You were in a casket,' I said. 'A glittering one, and so was Robbie. You were both dead.' Denie looked at me and a high titter of glee split our tension. I'd actually forgotten about Reeboks for a moment.

'Way to go, Meatgrinder, in a coffin, where she belongs. Denie, go bug someone else!' His glasses glinted and his teeth flashed as he jeered.

'Creep!' hissed Denie at him and swung her bike round. Then she looked at me, saw I wasn't laughing and that space-time blackness joined us for a moment. She cycled off and I shut my eyes, wanting to be very rude to Reeboks. But he was my only friend right now and I had Mum to think about. He was still speaking, breathless and quick, chewing gum.

'Connal, don't say anything, just look stupid, you can do that easy.' He caught my look and went on very quickly. 'I mean you're smart enough to look really stupid without anyone knowing.'

'Thanks, Reeboks,' I said.

I sat on my bike, thinking. Down the road, there was a car parked outside our house. It was a Holden, looking very ordinary, but I knew there was a cop in our house. Reeboks was right, it was time to do my stupid act. So I biked on down to our house. Yes, the Holden looked very ordinary with one side panel dented. There were no handcuffs or guns inside and I let my bike run slowly down through the gate to the door.

The guy inside looked ordinary, too. He was sitting on the couch, just where Roger had sat earlier, and was drinking coffee. Mum had shut the shop early and was looking uptight. She's just given up smoking, but this looked a different uptight from that. My mum is a fighter, big with frizzy brown-red hair, and she gets all her clothes from a second-hand place. Her uptight look was *scared* and that made me even more angry, so I put on an even more dumb expression as I faced the cop.

'Hi, Connal,' he said. 'I'm Sergeant Kepa.'

He had black hair, brown eyes and would have looked OK if he hadn't been a cop. I sat opposite and let the cop finish his coffee and put the cup gently down.

'Where did you spend last night, Connal?'

'Just out. I often go out,' I said quickly and added just to show the guy, 'Ask Reeboks – his dad's a bank manager.'

'I was here yesterday,' he said in a patient, smiling way. 'You shot out pretty quick.'

'Who says I had to hang round?'

Sergeant Kepa nodded, his brown eyes a bit sharp like Ms Booth when she's on to me in class. I superglued her desk once and she's never forgotten – she always looks at me sharply the way Sergeant Kepa was now. 'What'd you have in the bag, Connal?'

'Just some stuff, my stuff, so what's the problem?' I had my stupid look tight in place but his sharp grin seemed to cut through it. Cops who grin like that are not to be trusted.

'Do you like Roger?'

'He's OK,' I said carefully. 'He knew Dad.'

'I knew your dad, too,' said the sergeant. 'His songs anyway. I've got one of his tapes.'

Maybe he did, because Dad was on his way to the top

and had two tapes out. I was always playing mine and they were getting scratchy. Thinking about Dad must have made my face change again because Sergeant Kepa said gently, 'He was a good singer.'

I went into dumb mode. 'Yeah, and Roger was his mate.'

'Maybe.' Kepa gave me the full blast of his brown eyes. 'But that guy is dangerous, Connal, he's scum.'

'If you know that, then put him in jail.'

'Evidence,' said Kepa, 'we need evidence. The guy is dangerous, and we know he made some big scores. Did you see his loot anywhere?'

'Tell him, Connal, if you did,' said Mum. She still looked uptight and must have been thinking about her mortgage. I had to help her, so I shrugged and looked very stupid again.

'No. His gear's in the spare room.'

I didn't look at the sergeant. But he just waited and waited, then spoke slowly and gently like Ms Booth when she spells something out. 'Roger Blake is a dangerous thug. We want to put him away. But we need evidence.'

'Go on, Connal, tell him what you know,' said my mum.

I know you'll lose the mortgage, Mum, and I know these cops don't care, I thought, even if this guy was a fan of my dad's. This time I looked right into Sergeant Kepa's sharp brown eyes. 'I didn't see anything, sergeant.'

He looked at me, finished his coffee and got up to go. 'Mrs Burkitt, we can't hold Blake without evidence.' Mum nodded and he gave me a 'Catch you later, Connal' as he left. I hoped 'catch' didn't mean what I thought it did.

Mum had closed the shop. She stuck dinner in the microwave and we had it on our knees. Normally she then watched telly and went to bed early; I like Mum, but she spends a lot of time working. Then she said, 'What d'you know about this, Connal?'

'Mum, if the cops knew anything,' I said carefully, 'then they'd keep Roger in jail.'

She just muttered, 'I only let him in the house because—'

She stopped and I yelled out loud. 'Are you saying this was all my fault?' Suddenly I was angry, not with her but with all this incredible scaring trouble. 'Because I like to meet people who knew Dad? We should have gone on those trips with him and that was *your* fault!'

Normally Mum shouts back because she gets really tough sometimes. This time she just sat there silently and I slammed off angrily into my bedroom. I'd never said that to Mum before, even though I'd thought it enough times and it all came out like a flame-thrower going off. I sat on my bed, shutting my eyes tight and willing myself to wake up and fight some real battles on Deepwater – but when I opened my eyes it was still my room, with the plastic spiders and skeletons everywhere. I used to love all that swords and fantasy stuff and I really prized my American army helmet. Now I just tore everything down, stuffed it in the helmet and kicked it into a corner. Over my bed was a poster of one of Dad's tours and my big framed photo of him and his sombrero. It was white with an imitation rattlesnake headband and feather and I took it off the wall and put it on my head to help me think. I did this sometimes on special occasions. But I couldn't think about anything – my thoughts just crashed together and broke into pieces. I jammed the sombrero over my face, squeezed my eyes tight and tried to think of *anything* nice.

The broken pieces of my thoughts were zooming into black space. I thought about the kloppers – where had they come from? And why did I get such a real, *real* feeling when I thought about that crazy Deepwater dream? The room spun for a moment and I felt real giddy. Then, like a star in the blackness, I remembered Chibbi. Chibbi was nice, she'd listened, so I took off the sombrero and stood up. Her telephone number was in my pocket.

I went out into the hall. There was no sound from the living-room, but the telly was on with one of Mum's favourite soaps. Just like her, I thought, she's switched on when I left and had probably forgotten about me by now. I dialled Chibbi's number and her voice answered. It was her answer-phone, telling me to speak after I heard the beep noise. I don't like answer-phones, but I had to talk to someone, even if it was only a recording.

'Hi, Chibbi. This is Connal, who came to see you. I'd like to see you again because I had that Deepwater dream again. There were Martian monsters on Earth and the spaceship took off again, but I don't know where it's going.'

I gave her our number, put the phone down and went back into my room. I was going to sit down on my bed again when Dad's sombrero landed beside me and a deep voice said, 'Hi, Conny-boy.'

Conny-boy, was what Dad called me. They never found his body so always, somehow, I'd thought he might come back, but screwing my head round to look at the guy standing behind me took everything I had.

It was Roger. Roger the Ramraider.

He was standing over me, the window open behind him and his teeth gleaming like a dog-snarl in the darkness. 'Who were you calling, Connal?'

'Just a mate about going somewhere tomorrow.'

Roger's teeth kept gleaming, but he spoke softly. 'Sorry about that scare. Cops might be sniffing around.' He sat down on the end of the bed and looked round. 'That's a great poster of your dad.' It was the only poster from Dad's tours that I ever managed to get.

'You've seen it before.'

'Where's the gear, Connal?'

'I hid it.' My head spun a bit and my voice echoed. 'The cops don't know.'

'Nice work,' said Roger. 'So where is it?'

His grin seemed bigger somehow for a moment, making the room full of white teeth. I looked at him although my head felt heavy and my voice echoed again like I was back in that huge NUN chamber on the spaceship. So I had to shout, to make myself heard in the echoing darkness opening round me. 'I'll give it back to you. But you've got to go, leave me and Mum and never come back. Otherwise the cops will get it.'

I couldn't see Roger's face any more. His grin was part of the whirling, flashing darkness. I could feel his hand on my shoulder, though, and thought I heard my name . . . 'Connal . . . Connal . . . Conn . . .' and that was wrong because nobody on Earth called me Conn. Yoona did, though, but Yoona was on Deepwater; then I realised the voice was hers and opened my eyes.

I was back on Deepwater, but there was a storm of light and fire raging around me.

5   Stormlight in Deepwater

I was strapped to one of the control chairs. It was night outside Deepwater and we had stopped moving. Bren was in the control chair beside me and gave me a grim little smile, but didn't say anything. They all knew about prexing and they never talked about it. Yoona smiled down at me, pressing a thick blue biscuit and small round bottle into my hands.

'Our food and water dispensers are working again,' she said.

The biscuit tasted like thick, sweet chalk. Pressing the ribbed sides of the bottle shot a thin jet of water into my mouth. I rubbed some water over my face. There was this funny shut-down feeling in my mind as though being locked into this dream-state made Mum, Kepa and Reeboks all seem distant and unreal.

'How do you like the view?' said Bren.

'It's black,' I muttered.

'Deep space,' said Yoona. 'Those are stars.'

I just looked ahead into the black. Deepwater was moving so fast that we couldn't feel it. And into the blackness through the eye-windows came a shining dot of light, then another and another and they all shone bright and strong.

'I thought stars twinkled,' I muttered.

'Only from Earth,' said Yoona. 'The light gets caught between layers of atmosphere.'

'If you want to be on the crew of Deepwater, you have to know about space,' growled Bren. He was right, just

41

telling me what I had to know. Then a sudden flash of light made me blink. 'What was that?' I said.

'Static,' said Bren.

A set of glowing lights zapped suddenly across the consoles and Bren snatched his hands away. They danced off into the air round us, glowing specks of silver-white and black that bounced at each other like tennis balls.

'Starting again, Yoona,' he said.

The silver and black light-balls clashed and spread their flashing static into the air. I ducked as something like cold fire splashed against my cheek. 'We have some manual control,' said Yoona calmly, 'but COL is not answering and I haven't got a course bearing yet. All that static stops us using the consoles.' She pulled me up. 'Control is with you, Bren. Conn and I are going below.'

There was more static playing on the walls below and those silver and black balls seemed to follow us and set up their own dancing light. Gret and Lis lay on their bunks, asleep with that complete-exhaustion look, and it hit me that I'd never seen Yoona asleep. She pulled a long shining box out from under one of the bunks and opened it. 'Look at these, Conn.'

Inside the box were hundreds of little things like nails with crystal heads. The crystal light flashed in the static atmosphere and I remembered seeing them in that winding tunnel. I picked one up and cupped it in my hand. 'What are they?' I said.

'Gene capsules,' said Yoona softly. 'There's a life in each of these. See?' She pressed the crystal point and a hologram-picture flickered into life above it. It was a man's face, African with short dark hair, and smiling. I picked up one and pressed it. A European woman's face with long curly hair. Yoona replaced the capsules and closed the lid, placing the box in my hands.

'You're holding the human race, Conn,' she said. 'Human life on our planet, all that's left.'

'How do you make them work?' I whispered back.

'We don't know,' said Yoona. 'There must have been a programme lost on the other Deepwater.'

'You're all incredible,' I said. More of the light-balls danced and floated in the air, hovering over the sleeping faces of Gret and Lis. 'I still feel out of place here.'

Yoona closed the box and put it away. Then she took my hand in a very tight grip. 'No, you're in place, Connal. Denie's casket opened for a reason and so did yours. Denie taught us things and so will you.'

'Like who's causing this?' I said, flipping my hand through a light-ball.

Yoona looked at me, flinching slightly as a sharp flash of static sparked up the metal wall like a glowing cobweb. 'OK, what do you think?'

I hadn't really meant it. I opened my mouth to say 'nothing' when that little buzz hit me just under the tongue and other words came out. 'Maybe NUN's doing it. NUN could create holograms.'

Yoona just stared at me. 'What made you say that?'

'It just came out.'

Yoona crossed over quickly to the intercom. 'Bren, we're checking the NUN chamber. Call me on the remote if anything happens.' She clicked off and beckoned to me, walking quickly over to the far door. I followed, suddenly feeling more scared.

'I don't have to be right.'

'No?' Yoona was taking two laser rifles from a rack and handed me one. 'Conn, I never told you that NUN made holograms.'

There was more of the light force inside the long corridor that led to the NUN chamber. Black-patched on white, but with them a muddy drifting red and sparkling green. The lights were working and once a long flash of static ran alongside the wall, making the corridor glare white all along its length to the big door at the end.

'What are those symbols on the NUN door?' I whispered and another flash of yellow-red static speared down the corridor.

'Earth, fire, water, symbols of life,' said Yoona and whispered a quick instruction on how to use the laser rifle.

'What do you think we'll find in there?' I said.

'Shouldn't find anything,' said Yoona. She kept a rifle out front and her face was set in a tense scowl. 'You saw it empty. Zak smashed its terminal and Denie destroyed its life-force.'

'If you had to destroy it twice,' I said, 'it must take a lot of killing.' Another long spear of red static shot between us like a snake's fang. 'Maybe you can't destroy NUN till its programme is completed,' I said.

Yoona turned to face me again and this time there was a look in her eyes I hadn't seen before. Again she asked, 'What made you say that, Conn? How do you *know*?'

'I don't know. I'm just guessing,' I said. The static splattered again and another long tongue of red light unrolled up the corridor towards us. It moved almost lazily, then sprang at the last moment and jetted silently overhead.

'Then let's find out,' she said, scowling with determination.

We were nearly at the end now and the static light force seemed to explode in intensity. That door could only be opened by the palm-print of one of the crew. It stopped NUN's powers going beyond the NUN chamber. Yoona made to press her hand, but stopped and motioned me to. I knew why. She wanted to see if the systems of the ship accepted me. I pressed my palm against the enclosed ring of symbols. Something clicked and the door swung open.

We were back in the NUN chamber, but it was very different from the last time we'd seen it. Then it was a lonely, plain place. Now it was filled with all the static and it was as though we were entering another world with its own storm clouds and tempests. The light-balls danced at our level, while further up the static streaks whooshed into each other in mixing patterns of red and yellow. And high above, thick clouds and heavy coils like pythons came together in red, yellow, white and black thunder-claps that sent light-balls sleeting down like hail-storms. They twirled and looped in the air and sometimes one of them came streaking down. One was like a long yellow snake, coming straight at us and complete with open fanged jaws. Another snake, white, shot down and looped round it, pulling it back. The huge NUN chamber itself was rumbling and shaking to the awesome shimmering power around us.

Yoona looked round, her blonde-and-red hair streaming behind her as a wind-force took it. 'It's like ... like two electrical forces reacting to each other,' she said.

'Fighting each other?' I whispered.

Yoona shook her head, sending her hair flying again. Laser rifle out front, she began walking forward. I followed, the electronic storm wind tugging at my track suit and punching against my face. Another long streak of yellow storm fire whiplashed down and I felt the chill of a cold ice-fire. A shrill howling sound opened round us for a moment, splitting the air like the cold fire itself. It was as though a million screaming demons were fighting overhead.

In the centre now were the row of caskets, five open and three shut. The storm fire was playing and sparkling all over them and overhead it seemed to close and thicken like bad weather getting worse. Just for a moment, I thought I saw something squatting on one of the closed coffins.

'What's that thing?' I yelled.

Yoona looked, but the light force had whiplashed and the thing was gone. She shook her head, her long hair flying in the force, then yelled and pointed up.

Something large and almost boomerang-shaped was dropping down from the tumbling storm clouds above. Yoona pushed me aside, jumping back, pointing her rifle and almost stumbling in her haste to get ready. It was the first time I'd seen her off balance and really scared.

'Trites!' she screamed.

She thumbed the base of her laser and a streak of yellow light hissed up at the boomerang-wing thing. There was a sharp cracking sound as the laser split the electric-charged air before the yellow light speared thinly through the swooping thing. It didn't stop and Yoona fired again, but the yellow light again seemed to pass right through it. Then the thing was on her face, suddenly growing legs and wings as it gripped and I snatched at it. My fingers went through like grabbing cold jelly and the next moment it disappeared.

Yoona was shaking and pale, as though ready to collapse. Trites were the things these kids hated and feared. 'I thought they only lived in deep space,' I muttered, looking round with my own rifle ready.

'Solid-hologram,' said Yoona. 'Impossible, though, NUN's gone—' then she broke off, snapping her rifle down to the ready as something large and scaled slithered into view ahead, slipping through the stabbing light-beams like a snake through weeds.

'What's *that* thing?' I asked.

'Ice-worm, I think . . .' said Yoona uncertainly. 'Martian life-form, but . . .' She was going to say 'NUN's gone' again, but broke off as the overhead thunder-light split and crackled again and from the mixing light-mist came more fantastic shapes. Something bat-winged appeared for a moment and more of the boomerang things came swooping down. Yoona and I both fired at the same time, our laser hiss splitting the electronic storm forces, but they just kept coming, one of them so low that it flew through my up-pointing laser barrel. Another flew at Yoona's face; she flung up her gun barrel and squeezed her eyes shut, but it flew on and disappeared in the storm forces round us.

'It's OK, Conn, they can't hurt us,' said Yoona. The shrill howling noise came back and rose in intensity, like a hurricane, as the overhead forces crackled and smashed against each other like yellow-and-black-coloured fists. 'Come on.' She went forward, the light force streaming her hair.

'Shouldn't we tell the others?' I yelled into the force. It was blowing even harder now.

'I want to see where this goes,' she yelled back.

We were nearly halfway now. The wind howled even more strongly and tore at our clothes. More trites swooped and we ducked. There was something too real about them. 'If NUN is gone, what's making these?' I yelled.

Yoona stopped and let me come up. 'Maybe all this static is somehow reacting to its own circuits,' she said. 'Conn, why don't you go back? I'll be all right.'

'No way!' I yelled and she grinned, with a quick punch at my arm. It was like getting a medal.

Directly overhead now was the shattered remains of the NUN globe, the massive golden glove terminal that had once controlled their every movement. We couldn't see it because the light force was too thick, like a rushing whirlpool, but red, yellow and black-white light was zapping through and all over the row of caskets. It was still painful and unreal thinking about Robbie and Denie and I paused again. Yoona must have read my thoughts, shouting again above the noise. 'I know how you feel, Conn. But we have to go on!'

Now the light was dimming. A long slithering thing seemed to wind between the caskets. The lights dimmed further and beyond the caskets stood a motionless man-like shape. I stopped again, nudging Yoona, and pointed with my rifle barrel.

'Klopper!' I yelled.

The man-shape shambled forward, long arms to sides and seeming to ignore the storm winds screaming round it. We both had our rifles out, but the thing was not armed, even with a spear. It just kept coming, the face horribly smudged somehow, until the tip of Yoona's laser rifle pushed into its stomach and it scattered into a million glowing spots, torn away in the storm wind like sand.

'Something's playing games with us,' yelled Yoona. 'NUN, or—'

She broke off again, because out of the storm force more of the klopper-holograms were advancing from the other side of the caskets. We stood watching, waiting for them to come up and disappear, when something hit me like that little buzz under my tongue. Maybe it was the way they were walking into the storm forces without the forces seeming to slow them down, or the weapons this lot held, but I yelled to Yoona. 'They're alive!'

As I pushed her back, a crossbow bolt skimmed past my cheek. That was no hologram! I raised my laser rifle, but Yoona knocked it up, pushing me back. We turned and ran to the door.

At first it was easy because we were running with the light force at our backs. Then suddenly it changed and beat towards us, so now we were staggering into a storm and horrible hologram shapes flickered round us, creatures from a long-ago Martian nightmare. We staggered on and I looked back.

Behind us, the kloppers were advancing in an unhurried line. Maybe their big feet couldn't move fast, but as I watched one raised its crossbow and the bolt whizzed over our heads. They were still bad shots.

We were nearly at the door and the storm forces still raged hard, as though not wanting to let us go. Strong red and yellow electric fingers grabbed at us, the fingers became a slamming fist. A spear clinked on the door as Yoona opened it, another one sailed down the corridor between us and we were through. The olive-green tank-figures were almost at our heels when Yoona slammed the door and silence descended.

'We're OK now,' gasped Yoona. 'Not even NUN can

open that door.' She pressed her back to it, breathless and panting hard. 'How did you know they were real ones?'

'I didn't.' It was true, I didn't. 'Just something inside me.'

'Good instinct,' said Yoona, still breathless. Ahead, the corridor still stormed with static and light-balls, but we somehow knew they were not dangerous. 'So where did that lot come from?'

'Dunno,' I said. 'Was NUN making them?'

It was Yoona's turn to not know. She walked down the corridor and picked up the spear, passing her hand down the long shaft and looking at me, puzzled.

'Conn, this doesn't make sense.' She went on, talking to herself. 'NUN is dead, NUN is burned out.'

'Are you sure?' I asked.

Yoona made to nod, then stopped herself. It was only the second time I'd seen it and it gave me a creeping, scared feeling again. Fear.

'No,' she said, 'I'm not sure of anything now.'

6 Evil inside, evil outside

'NUN? Coming back to life? Impossible.' Lis summed it up for all of them. Yoona had woken her and Gret and we were all on the control deck, and the way Lis said it was how they all felt – scared and incredulous.

'Something else might be activating the circuits,' said Yoona. 'A power surge perhaps.'

'The same power surge that's taking us nowhere?' muttered Gret. She was beside Bren and both were frowning at Yoona.

'We don't know,' said Yoona.

'And COL's not activated either,' said Lis. 'So what *is* driving Deepwater?'

Nobody knew the answer to that. Outside there were stars, near and distant, but until we worked out a fix on them we couldn't tell which was which. The kids passed the klopper spear from hand to hand and although they were very tough, they were all quiet and scared.

'NUN was terminated,' said Lis, breaking the silence. 'Twice.' Then she pressed her blue lips together, realising how silly it was to say anything was terminated twice.

Round us, the same spider-webs of energy were playing up the walls and over the ceiling, crackling energy round us. The light-balls still hung in the air, coming together, popping and then exploding back into life. Yoona was standing by the main COL console and her hand kept going to it as though wanting – wishing – that her own energy would bring it back to life.

'So how did the kloppers get on to the ship?' said Bren.

I remembered those olive-green shapes running through the undergrowth before the ship took off. 'Something let them,' I said. 'But why didn't the same thing let them on before, when they were *trying* to get in?' The energy web flashed again and a loud vibrating hum ran through the control deck.

'No,' said Lis. 'Deepwater has defence systems to zap anything alien. The kloppers would have been zapped too.' She stopped, thinking hard, running her hands through her blue hair. 'So how *did* they get in?'

I was still having that funny little buzz under my tongue like a radio being tuned to a new wave-length. The buzzing noise sharpened painfully, then died away. 'Maybe they weren't trying to keep us in,' I said. It sounded like I was pushing the words out.

There was silence, but for the sharp-split buzzing hum of static, and it reflected in Gret's green face as she spoke. 'Why do you say that?'

'Because the kloppers must have got on to the ship somehow,' replied Yoona quietly.

I didn't say anything, but there was something buzzing in my head, so sharply, so complex and strange that I couldn't put it into words.

'Take-over,' I said.

'What d'you mean, take-over?' said Yoona.

The static was buzzing painfully under my tongue and through my head. I remembered the kloppers out in Earth-forest and inside the NUN chamber. They should have caught us but they didn't, they should have stuck us full of bolts and spears – but they didn't.

'I don't know about kloppers,' I said, feeling a dizzy spell come over me. 'Tell me what they are.'

Yoona didn't answer, but Lis did. 'Kloppers, Mars, pre-colonisation life-form, died out about a million years ago, before humans. They developed big lungs to hold the thin air, they were flesh-eaters, became extinct about 500,000 BC.' Before Colonisation, she meant.

So Mars was practically airless when the kloppers died out, I thought. 'Could they live without air for a time?'

'Store air in their lungs?' said Lis.

Yoona shrugged, closing her eyes for a moment. 'Maybe.' Then she opened them wide as she realised what I was saying. 'Yes, they could!'

I think they were all clicking then. The kloppers and whoever was controlling them, wanted control of Deepwater. They couldn't get through the NUN chamber and there was only one other way. They all realised what it was at the same time.

'Space suits!' yelled Yoona.

These were in lockers at the other end of the deck. We scrambled into them quickly, Lis helping me with mine, and Yoona used the manual controls to seal the lower deck. Gret and Bren were already moving towards the spiral staircase that led to the broken bubble and Lis elbowed them angrily. 'That's my station, come on, Conn.'

'You can't take a prexing Earthkid,' shouted Gret into her intercom.

'I'll go with you, Lis,' shouted Yoona.

'You're voice-activated to COL, it might come back on-line,' replied Lis, grabbing me firmly by the arm. She was at the upper hatch now, pressing the button to unseal.

'Conn, be careful,' came Yoona's voice in my intercom.

'Hold tight,' said Lis as she pushed the hatch open.

I grabbed the sides of the staircase as the air rushed out in a brief blast and Lis trod on my gloved hand as she scrambled out. The space suits were thick and clumsy, but became magically light in zero pressure. Below, helmeted faces looked up as I scrambled out of the hatch after Lis into the shattered circle of glass that was once the bubble-turret.

We were only just in time.

Coming up the back of Deepwater was a line of kloppers. They had spears and crossbows and what looked like magnetic plates strapped to their feet. Somebody or something had done a good job of preparing them and they looked fantastic, like sword and fantasy warriors marching up the silver-plate motorway that was Deepwater's back. With the turret room smashed, they could have opened the hatches from the other side and come in. Even if the sudden depressurisation didn't kill us, we would've been outnumbered because there were more than fifty of them.

They were walking solidly, clumping up in a line, the thick lips tight shut and the heavy-lidded eyes glaring at us. And they were nearly there, nearly on top of us. I just stood there, but Lis knew just what she was going to do. She was pulling me towards the big laser cannon, pushing me into a recliner chair. 'Yoona said it can't fire,' I gasped.

'Other ways to make it work,' came Lis's voice in my intercom and I could see her grin behind the visor. She had her hands on the controls and worked her metal-soled flight boots into the pedals. A bolt whizzed past us as she did so. The kloppers were nearly at the shattered glass circle now, holding out their spears like a giant spiked broom, ready to sweep us out of the gun-chair. Lis laughed again and shouted through the intercom. 'Hold tight, Conn.'

She was working the controls to lower the two long gun barrels of the laser until they were pointing straight ahead. Then she began to spin it round, working the manual controls and sweeping the twin barrels in a wide circle.

The kloppers stopped just in time. The gun barrels would have swept them off Deepwater like skittles. Some bolts and spears shot at us in the blackness, but we were sheltered by the gun and Lis set a pattern, sweeping it back and forth and laughing as she did. 'Come on,' she shouted. 'Who wants their ugly skull dented first?'

The kloppers stopped, still tight-lipped, showing no emotion. The long barrels swung back and forth like a pair of wheel-spokes, knocking pieces of glass off. They twirled slowly into the air like upward shining star pieces, but between the gun barrels and the rest of the glass, there was no way for a klopper to get past. One threw a spear, but it just sailed slowly past us.

It was an incredible and fantastic sight – that line of scowling green faces and Lis laughing in the intercom as she swung the gun round. Overhead, the blackness stretched endlessly. And everywhere, like bright white burning jewels, were the stars, single and in groups, some close, some flung round in distant clusters and on its own, burning yellow as gold, the sun. It was all wonderful, beautiful and unreal, even with the danger of the kloppers and the same unreality of Lis laughing through the intercom as she worked the gun barrels to keep them away. Yoona's voice came through the intercom, tense and hurried.

'OK, Lis, welding equipment in place, disengage when you're ready.'

'No hurry,' said Lis, grinning through her helmet at me. 'We're enjoying the exercise.'

Already the kloppers were backing off. They could hold air in their lungs for a very long time, but they had a long way to go back to whichever part of Deepwater they came from. Their leader scowled round at them, but didn't dare open his mouth to call them back – all the air would have been shot out of his lungs. He was the one in the crude leather harness with the big shells on either side. He pressed his lips together and scowled even harder, trying to jab forward with his spear. It was nearly knocked from his hand.

'Come on,' came Yoona's voice again.

The other kloppers had given up. So did the klopper leader with a last glare at us, and Lis began slowing the gun barrels down. The klopper leader turned and, with a surprising speed, put one clawed foot on the glass and tried to scramble over. Lis swept the gun and a red streak appeared on his green leg as the iron-glass cut him, but he was over.

55

One gun barrel hit him but instead of being knocked off, he grabbed it and was whirled round, legs kicking in the black stillness.

Lis's face was set and grim behind her visor now. She began to raise the barrel to full elevation and the klopper hung on grimly. I knew what she'd do, just slam it back down again and knock him off – or stick him on the iron-glass. She was already lowering it when that little buzz went off under my tongue.

'No!'

'What?' she yelled.

I scrambled out of the recliner and under the gun barrel, making it impossible for Lis to lower it any further. I grabbed the klopper's spear and reached up to grab his foot and pull him down. He looked at me, the tight-lipped, slit-eyes expression staying in place; there was no sign of fear, or even of asking to be helped. I pulled him down the gun barrel, keeping the spear pointed, and he understood all right. One little poke and he would be out into space for ever.

Lis looked at me, not frowning now, but puzzled. Starlight danced off the visor of her helmet as she clumped back over to the hatch and opened it. I prodded the klopper ahead and it followed her. Lis gave me a last look back and shook her head inside the helmet, then went down. I motioned the klopper to follow, wondering what the others would think when they saw that big four-clawed foot appear on the stairs. It glared at me, scowling as much as its tight lips would let it, and went down. All the other kloppers were well down the silver-plate road of Deepwater, without looking back. So much for loyalty, I thought, and followed the klopper down.

Nobody spoke into their intercoms as I came through. The hatch shut and Bren just gave me the same puzzled, frowning look that Lis did as he cut the torch into action and began welding the bolts permanently shut. The klopper was at the bottom and Gret had her laser rifle on him.

The silence went on as Yoona reopened the lower deck hatch. Air and the gravity force that COL somehow made came flooding through and restored pressure. The klopper stood there by the stairway, claw-hands clenched and eyes in heavy-lidded slits. I knew that pose, I'd even done it myself the time Ms Booth caught me standing over kids for their lunch money. He was acting tough and feeling scared. He let out a long sighing gasp of air and began to breathe, his big scaly-green chest moving up and down. There was a click-click round us as the others raised their visors, hostile anger seeming to come into the deck with the air.

'What did you bring *that* in for?' said Gret in a hard voice.

'Point it in the direction of the airlock,' growled Bren over the hiss of the welding torch.

'Why, Conn . . . ?' said Lis, still sounding puzzled.

Then a helmet hit the metal floor of the control deck with a loud clang and we all looked over. Just for a moment we had forgotten Yoona, maybe because she had stayed so quiet. But we all knew just what she was thinking. It was in her yellow eyes, as hard and flashing as jewels, in the tight set of her wide mouth and how she walked forward to take Gret's laser and thumb off the safety-catch for firing.

'Get out of the way, Conn,' she said. Her eyes narrowed to fierce slits and her voice was tight-cold in a way I'd never heard before.

'We can't kill it,' I said.

'These things killed Reb and Cei!' yelled Yoona and her eyes blazed like brown-gold sun-fire. 'Stand aside!'

Now there were tears of rage in her eyes and the others stood silent, apart from the hissing of Bren's torch. I'd never seen her in such a cold rage, but made myself stand in front of the klopper. He was motionless, like an olive-green statue, but I could feel a little shaking feeling for him; kloppers were afraid of death and that somehow made him more human. 'You can't do this, Yoona,' I said.

She advanced on me until the muzzle of her laser was close to my chest. 'Stand aside or I'll fire through you.'

'Robbie and Denie would love that,' I said.

'I mean it,' she whispered, the sound of Bren's torch making her words hiss.

She did, too. She was in command, she gave the orders and I was in the way. No captain can let one of the crew defy them. She would do it – she was tough enough to – and I had just moments to think. I stepped up to her and the laser rifle touched my chest. Yoona did not step back at all and her eyes shone with that angry glare. I looked away, over my shoulder and up to the klopper, speaking loud so that everyone could hear me.

'Why did you kill Denie and Robbie?'

'Not mean to,' grunted the klopper, eyes still slit with tension.

That was a shock for everyone, even Yoona. None of them had heard kloppers speaking except me. It grunted the words in a rough, basic way, but still they were clear. And so was Yoona's intent from her next words. Her gun barrel still prodded into my chest as she spoke, whispering the words in that same hard-hissing way. 'You shot them with crossbow bolts. I saw the wounds and the blood!' The nightmare of that made her words blood-sticky too.

'Not mean to,' grunted the klopper again, his olive-green body still shaking behind me in a funny immobile way. As scared as any human, as scared as me.

'Why?' I asked and that little static-buzz crept under my tongue. 'What were your orders?'

'Orders?' whispered Lis incredulously.

'Keep you on Deepwater.'

The klopper grunted the words, but they were clear enough and were heard by everyone – so close to what I'd said before that even Yoona blinked and her laser rifle wavered for a moment. She was still flushed, though, very cold and angry, her yellow eyes like hot stones. She was as tense and deadly as a fully-strung crossbow.

'Keep us on Deepwater?' I said it softly because Yoona's rifle was still touching my chest.

The klopper looked sullenly at us, like the time I was caught smoking behind the bike shed by two teachers. 'Told to,' it said.

'*Told to*?' yelled Yoona. '*Who* told you to? And who said kill Reb and Cei by *accident*?'

'And who's telling you to kill it – on purpose?' I yelled back.

'They're animals, Conn.'

'So what does that make you, Yoona?'

For a moment I thought she was going to shoot the klopper through me. Then something came into her eyes, something that was trying to understand through the anger. And although I didn't like Gret much, I could never thank her enough for coming in when she did.

'Where on Deepwater do you come from?' she said to the klopper. 'Where've you been hiding?'

'Down,' said the klopper and one four-clawed hand unclenched to point at the floor. 'Where demons are.' Then the klopper struggled because it was trying to think, trying to make *us* think. 'We on Deepwater – like you.'

Their spaceship as well as ours. That was so stunning that even Bren flicked off his hissing torch for a moment. There was just the harsh panting breath of the klopper, deadly scared, when Lis spoke up like a little blue hero.

'Wrong, Yoona,' she said.

There was a total silence. I did not believe it, but Gret came over, scowling in her green way. Yoona took a step back. They were defying her, *all* of them, and she knew she was wrong. I never realised what it was like being commander until Yoona took another step back and let her rifle fall. Not because she was weak, but because she was back in control. Because she knew what was right. 'Yes,' she said to the klopper in a voice that still caught. 'So who told you to keep us on Deepwater?'

'Who told you?' repeated Lis, looking up. 'We won't hurt you, so tell us.'

'Didn't want to,' said the klopper, standing like olive-green stone. 'Tried to get away from being told. Demons stopped us.' I could smell the fear and a sense that this thing wasn't as stupid as it looked. The claw-hands clenched and unclenched and the heavy-lidded eyes blinked. That little static-buzz came under my tongue and tingled my body as I looked straight into the klopper's tense face.

'Was it NUN?' I asked. 'NUN told you to?'

The klopper's mouth widened and it opened its mouth to speak. Then suddenly, the static electricity exploded into life. A burst of jagged yellow fire shot out of the wall, seeming to spear the klopper through, and it stiffened, crashing to the floor like a falling tree. I got down on my knees beside it and could hear faint hissing breath. It was still alive and I stood up to face Yoona.

'Do you still want to kill it?'

Yoona ran both hands through her hair, letting it fall around her face. She shook her head slightly, a dazed look in her eyes. 'Get that thing below,' she said.

Even with Gret and Bren dragging at the front and Lis at the heels, it took all three of them to get the klopper down the stairs. Yoona watched, blinked and drew a deep breath as though she was just out of deep water.

'I didn't know I could hate like that,' she said. 'You're right, Conn. Deepwater is a life mission, not the other way round.'

She went over to the control chair and sat down, looking at deep space and all those shining jewel-stars. I think that really it was the first time she was coming to terms with her own grief at Robbie and Denie's death; how easily that hate was itself a killer. I sat down beside her and after a minute she took me over Deepwater's controls, voice-activating me to the dead COL console, showing me how to run things, her way of saying 'Thanks, Conn'. Once she looked at me and gave a little twitchy smile and shut her eyes. Saying goodbye to Robbie was very hard and I let her do it. She opened them again when Lis, Bren and Gret came up from the lower deck. All their hate was gone, too, because they'd faced the klopper enemy and seen it was like them.

'What did that thing mean – down below?' asked Bren. 'There's nothing below but the Wingfish bay.' This is the launch bay for the big lifeboats that Deepwater carries, mini-spaceships of their own.

'That doesn't go all ways under the ship,' said Lis. 'We don't know what's under the rest of Deepwater.'

'I do,' said Yoona.

She sat up in her control chair and pointed ahead, sounding so certain that it sent a static-buzzing chill through me. Ahead was a small orange-red speck, and even at that distance I knew what it was. She was speaking now in quiet, rapid words, still pointing.

'It makes sense. The klopper pointed below and *must* be from a gene bank. So Deepwater did not have just one gene bank aboard, but *two*!' She gripped the sides of her chair and opened her eyes with a bright realising knowledge and a bitter laugh. 'We'd always thought Deepwater's final destination was Earth.' She swung round in her control chair. '*No*! Its final destination is the planet *where it came from*!' Her pointing finger was still centred on the small orange-red dot ahead of us. And even I knew what that planet was before Gret breathed the single incredulous word.

'Mars?'

The words caught like an echo in all their throats and everything swam giddily as Yoona spoke, as sharply as a klopper's hiss.

'Mars, yes, *Mars*!' yelled Yoona. 'Deepwater was launched by Martian colonists and therefore it ends at its *home planet*!' Her eyes blazed with the old fire. 'Of course the klopper comes from down there – because all this is pre-programmed, because we have a Martian gene bank on board and are taking it home.'

'Home?' echoed Lis.

I couldn't hold my dizziness any more and I knew that terrible prex-state was starting again. I sat down on the control chair, but the deck was spinning now and Lis's voice echoed again in the swirling blackness.

'Home is a dead planet.'

7   Roger and the knife

'Connal, are you OK?' my mum asked. She was standing over me, the sun was coming in through the bedroom windows behind her and I realised it was morning. Mum was dressed, still with that strained look on her face, and I sat up: I still had my clothes on.

'I couldn't wake you last night,' she said.

'I'm OK, Mum,' I replied.

I wasn't – my head was still spinning and I felt hot and sticky. Mum said something about breakfast and went out. I sat on my bed, thinking about Deepwater and Mars and how unreal all this was now, as though Reeboks, Roger the Ramraider and all my problems here were just a plastic dream. I washed and changed. There was something stuffed in one of my pockets, a stone with a note wrapped round it. It read, 'OK KID. DON'T CROSS ME.' The 'DON'T' was heavily underlined. I screwed it up and went out into the kitchen. Mum's assistant, Mrs Rasmussen, was in the shop, so she was still having breakfast. She put on toast for me and I poured cereal, thinking about the blue biscuits and sharp-tasting water on the spaceship.

'Don't worry about Roger,' she said. 'If he comes back, I'll chuck him out on his ear.'

She didn't know about last night or the note. I just shook my head. 'No, Mum, it's not him.'

Mum put her coffee down and put her arm a bit awkwardly round me. Mum and I never show much emotion. 'I know things have been rough, Connal. I'll try and make

63

them better.' I felt bad when she said that, because Mum usually worked a twelve-hour day in the shop.

'I'm OK, Mum, really.'

She looked at me and got up to go into the shop. She must have thought I was sulking and playing dumb, but I was close to tears. That scared me because I never cried, even when Dad died.

I felt like I belonged in two places at once. I couldn't handle this world, and on Deepwater things were getting too complex. My crewmates – that was the first time I'd called them that – were heading for a dead planet and with them, the gene stock that was supposed to repopulate planet Earth. Everything had gone horribly wrong and there were no answers anywhere. Mum appeared from the shop again.

'Connal, someone called Chibbi rang. Is she a girlfriend?' Mum hopes I'll find a nice girl, she says, to knock the corners off me, whatever that means.

'No, Mum. Wish she was.'

She was going out to the shop and paused at the door, sounding very awkward. 'Connal, there is nothing between me and Roger.'

'Did he really know Dad?' I asked.

Mum came a little more back in. Talking about Dad made her sad. 'Your dad moved round a lot and knew stacks of people. Trying to make our fortunes, he always said.' She sounded very sad.

'But you left him.' Unfair, but I bit off the words too late.

'I left him because I had a growing kid called Connal,' she said. 'I didn't want us to split up but he stopped coming home.'

'And I never saw him again!' I yelled. 'You did that!'

Mum looked at me, her face white. Her eyes stared; she opened and closed her mouth. I'll never know what would have happened next because Mrs Rasmussen came in from the shop. She had on a bright sari and the little

64

shining dot on her forehead over her nice brown eyes. 'Connal, your little friend Graeme is outside,' she said and went back into the shop.

Mum went out into the shop and I was so angry with myself that I nearly chucked my cereal bowl at the wall. I keep hurting Mum when I don't mean to. And I didn't want to see Reeboks, so I grabbed my jacket and ducked out the back, but he was already there. Reeboks is *very* smart.

'What's up, Connal?' he said, his mouth full of gum. 'Where're you going?'

I was going to see Chibbi. Then maybe I was going to take the cops to the creek near the storm-drain. But I wasn't telling Reeboks any of this and just said, 'Things to do, Graeme.'

'I'll see you later,' he shouted. 'By the creek?'

'Yeah, I'll be there,' I yelled back and forgot him as I quickly cycled off. It was all different this time because Deepwater was still real and everything round me was becoming unreal, as though painted on something. I biked up to the university and went through to where the lab was. I could hear a ukelele and someone singing. I knew Chibbi's voice.

'The olive tree stands in stony ground, but my true love waits beneath it,' she sang . . . 'The olive fruit lies on the ground, the leaves of the tree—'

Inside the lab, I stopped. Chibbi was there with Denie Miles, a bag of crisps and two juice cartons between them. Chibbi was cross-legged on the table and Denie on one of the lab stools, a big black hat slung on her back. Chibbi put down the ukelele.

'Hi, Connal. You and Denie know each other, don't you?'

I nodded. 'Sure.'

'Hi, Connal,' said Denie.

I looked at her smiling freckled face and it hit me again. On Deepwater, Denie was dead in a crystal casket, and on Earth she was smiling at me.

'Denie came in to say goodbye,' said Chibbi. 'I've been singing her a song I wrote but it doesn't translate from the Spanish.'

I nodded. Denie could see there was something wrong and some of her smile went as she looked at Chibbi. 'I have to go now and Mum says dinner is about seven.'

'I'll be there,' said Chibbi.

Denie jumped down, tipping the big hat over her face. 'D'you like it, Connal? Chibbi's goodbye present.'

'It looks great,' I said. Denie tipped the hat nearly over her eyes and left, whistling the tune of the folk song.

Chibbi let me sit down. She pushed the crisps towards me, but I just shook my head. 'Connal, you look like you saw a ghost,' she said.

'I did.' It wasn't the first time I'd looked at Denie like that. 'She and Robbie are dead on Deepwater. Those Martian things did it, but we caught one and he says it was an accident.'

Chibbi plucked a string on her ukelele. 'That was an incredible telephone message you left,' she said. 'All right, Connal, talk to me about it.'

I told her what had happened since we last met. Normally I find it hard to talk to people, but since this began, words came easily and it was good talking to Chibbi anyway. She just listened and my words zapped out, the right words, even long words in a way I'd never been able to talk before.

Chibbi didn't say anything. She had on faded blue jeans with flower-patches and a black T-shirt with the red splattered words 'Taco Sticko', and a white sleeveless jacket with red beads down the front. She hooked one finger in a red handkerchief tied round her neck and looked at me. 'Now tell me about your problems here.'

'Don't you believe me?' I shouted.

Chibbi just went on in the same calm voice. 'Denie has no memory of Deepwater any more and neither does Robbie. But they both know you have problems, Connal.'

'And does that make me a liar?'

'No, it makes you someone with problems,' she replied, just as calmly.

So I told her about my mum and my dad, about Roger the Ramraider, about Reeboks, the loot and Sergeant Kepa. At the end of it she paused again before giving a very long whistle and strumming more notes on the ukelele.

'You do know how to keep busy, don't you, Connal?'

Then she gave me such a great grin that I had to smile back. Chibbi began to laugh and I laughed too, the best thing that had happened in the last few days. Chibbi strummed a few more notes and her smile went.

'This Sergeant Kepa sounds regular,' she said. 'And you don't owe Roger anything, even if he was a mate of your dad's.'

'Dad would never want me getting his mates into trouble,' I said.

'Oh, your dad liked crims?' Chibbi asked. She waited until she saw the 'No!' shout started to form on my lips and went on, 'Roger has busted a lot of shops just like your mum's, little folk trying to make a buck. What about them, Connal?'

She was making me think, and I liked that. But I still had my problems, so I frowned to show her I wasn't easily fooled, even though I had the feeling she was seeing right through me. 'I've got to think about Mum. You know about the mortgage and stuff.'

'Reeboks doesn't sound like a friend to me,' said Chibbi, 'no matter how classy his shoes are.' She put the ukelele in her lap. 'Connal, it's your decision, but I think you should go to Sergeant Kepa.'

I couldn't understand this. Chibbi was talking about Earth-side and I was talking about Space-side. 'What about Deepwater and going to Mars?'

Chibbi laid her ukelele aside. 'Connal,' she said quietly, 'This happened to Robbie and Denie before you. And it's changed you . . . the same way it changed them. But Earth-side is important, too.'

'Space-side,' I muttered. 'What happens to Robbie, Denie and you?'

'Me?' said Chibbi, even more careful.

'You died in a Moon city in 2040,' I said. Straight away I hated myself for letting the words jet out over my tongue. There was a long, long silence before Chibbi took up her ukelele and played some more sad notes.

'Well, it's always good to know how long you've got,' she said, playing a few notes before putting the ukelele aside again.

'I'm just saying things are different,' I said, knowing my words were wandering off as though they were lost.

'Maybe more alike than you think,' said Chibbi and her eyes shone, her voice echoing as though she was speaking inside a huge chamber. 'So, follow your instinct. Promise?'

'Promise,' I heard myself saying.

'And hang loose,' she said. 'Look after yourself.'

I heard myself say 'Thanks, Chibbi,' and then I was leaving. She began to play the ukelele again, but sadly, thinking with her hands on the strings as Dad used to, as though thinking about trouble. I knew I was still headed for a lot of that.

When I got outside, the trouble started. My bike was missing and I groaned. Of all times for this to happen, somebody had stolen it. Then a station-wagon drew up alongside and the window came down.

'Your bike's in the back, kid. Get in.'

It was Roger. I didn't want to get in because the car was sure to be stolen, but I had to see this through. He took off, driving carefully, even stopping at the lights because the last thing Roger wanted was a traffic cop stopping him. 'Connal, I have a private plane waiting to take me to Australia. I need my gear and I need it now.'

68

'And you won't bother us again?'

He shook his head and I gave him directions to the park. Roger frowned a bit, glanced at me, but I didn't speak. I think he was puzzled and he finally said, 'Kid, we're mates, aren't we? Your dad and I were good mates, so what's the big problem now?'

'What about the people you ramraid?' I said.

'Business,' he said, and winked, but I just looked at him.

He pulled up the station-wagon and we got out. I pointed to where the bridge was and the storm-drain. 'There you are,' I said. 'Go and get it.' I pulled my bike out of the back.

'You go and get it,' he said. 'And no tricks.'

He opened up his jacket and sticking in his belt was the bone handle of a knife. Roger touched it and winked again in a cold and deadly way. I ran over to the bridge and knelt, feeling underneath, hooking my hand round the strap and pulling it out. Then I felt a real shock. Roger was standing just behind me, his hand inside his jacket. 'Got it, kid?' he asked.

I nodded. Roger was looking over my head and his good-looking face suddenly snarled like a dog. 'You little rat!' he yelled and turned, running. I could hear more running now, footsteps pounding up to us. Sergeant Kepa and two more cops were coming out of cover towards us. I couldn't let them find the jewels – that would be the end of Mum and me! So I turned and ran, the heavy bag dragging beside me.

'Stop, Connal, we know all about it,' I heard Kepa yell from behind.

I propped the bag on the handlebars of my bike and began to pedal hard. A quick look behind showed two cops chasing me, but the park sloped here and I put on speed. There was beach and sea about half a kilometre away and lots of places to dump the bag where it would never be found. I risked another look back and only one cop was chasing. The other was running back to where they must have parked their car. But I saw something else that made me chill.

Sergeant Kepa was chasing Roger, not me, and he was closing. Roger was nearly at the car but he had his hand under his belt again and I remembered the knife. I broadsided my bike round; the heavy bag slammed on the handlebars and it went down. I scrambled up, yelling, because suddenly the most important thing was not letting Sergeant Kepa be hurt.

'Sergeant – Sergeant, he's got a knife!'

Kepa stopped as Roger turned, raising his hand to throw. Something flashed and Kepa ducked, losing his balance and falling. Roger was diving into the station-wagon and he took off as the other came roaring into sight in his car, light and siren flashing. Both cars disappeared from sight and Kepa got up, walking slowly over to me, covered in mud. There was no expression on his face, but he bent over once to pick up something that flashed. Roger's knife. A third cop was up, too, and between them they opened the bag and looked inside. Jewels, watches, chains and everything shone up at them.

Still without expression, Sergeant Kepa looked at me. 'Where were you going with this?'

'To dump it, so Mum wouldn't get into trouble,' I said.

'You should've kept going, then,' he said. He passed the knife to the other cop, who whistled softly as he ran his finger down the blade.

I didn't say anything. I couldn't. He was a cop and would do his job, whatever. Sergeant Kepa looked at the other cop, who nodded slightly, took the bag and began walking back over the bridge. Kepa had his mouth set in a funny frown, like there was a little smile underneath it.

'You're not in trouble, Connal, and neither is your mum. You were returning this lot when we tangled with Roger.'

'I was running with it,' I said.

Sergeant Kepa let his little frown become more of a smile.

70

'No, Connal,' he said, 'you weren't.'

Sergeant Kepa drove me home. We parked and he tried to rub some of the mud off his clothes as we got out, muttering about what his wife would do to him. 'Connal, there's a big insurance reward for recovery of that stuff,' he said. 'I'll make sure you get half.' He rubbed at the mud again and added softly, 'And thanks for what you did back there.'

'I didn't want him to stick you with the knife,' I said.

'Neither did I,' he said, smiling. A message came over the car radio to say that Roger had got away and Kepa shrugged. 'He'll be on the plane by now. You're well rid of him.'

'Thanks, Sergeant,' I said.

He smiled again. 'I'll buy you a hamburger some time soon and we'll talk about ancestors. And play your dad's tape – OK?'

'OK,' I said.

He talked to Mum before he left. Mum never says much, but she hugged me tighter than she ever had until I had to tell her to let me go. 'The insurance money is yours, Connal,' she said.

'No, Mum, both of us,' I said – the wrong thing, because she hugged me even tighter. It was good, though, and so was the thought of the reward, but I couldn't help wondering who was getting the other half. Because somebody must have tipped off Kepa to watch the storm-drain area.

I don't remember much about the rest of the day. I had dinner early, went to my room and took Dad's hat down from over my bed. I put it on, feeling him close and knowing I hadn't done anything to make him ashamed of me. I got undressed and into bed because I wanted to get up early, go and talk to Denie, talk to Chibbi again, even talk to Sergeant Kepa about ancestors.

I had a strange feeling that Dad's big hat had glided off the wall and settled on my face. I thought about Denie's black hat, too, and everything went into darkness. Now the darkness was closer and, spinning, I knew what it was. I could feel my Earth-state memory draining like water out of a basin as the room spun round me and I felt myself being pulled back across space and time to the other reality of Deepwater.

I was strapped into one of the control chairs on the command deck of Deepwater. I kept my eyes shut, because I couldn't hear the others and there was a strange, rigid feeling to Deepwater and a sense of thick dust in the air that got up my nose. I sneezed and opened my eyes. A red sandy dust was drifting through the command deck like a gentle sandstorm and outside, through the eye-windows, was the roughest, strongest landscape I had ever seen.

It was mainly red, with huge slabs of rock tumbled unevenly against each other as though a giant had crashed them together. In the distance, a massive red mountain loomed and all over the red-orange rock was heaps of drifting sand, set with little green spiky cacti. Mars, I told myself, knowing it *had* to be – we had landed and were here on the dead planet.

Yoona, Bren and Gret were strapped in the other control chairs, muttering and stirring. Maybe the impact of landing had stunned them and the settling clouds of dust outside Deepwater showed it had only just happened. Just standing up was different, too, and so was breathing. The gravity was different, the air thinner and cold. I found out why as I went below deck, and why the dust was drifting through Deepwater. The landing impact must have somehow opened the airlock doors and I was breathing in real Martian air.

The dust hung more thickly here, outlining the strapped figure of the klopper and, two beds down, Lis. She was just coming to as well and I undid her straps and gently helped her to sit up. 'Are we here, Conn?' she whispered, 'On Mars?' She didn't say 'home', even though this planet was where her genes came from – because home was dead. Then I took another breath of that cold air and remembered the little green cacti. Mars *wasn't* dead and ... I stopped, because two beds down the klopper rolled his eyes in blinking fear, looking past us to the open airlocks.

A figure stood there in the drifting red dust-clouds – strange, two-legged, with a crazy crested head, walking up towards us. All of this was getting more and more incredible. The figure was covered in the reddish-orange dust and held a spear. But this wasn't the most crazy thing in this most crazy prex-awakening. It was a female person, blue-skinned like Lis, with one red arm and one red leg. Her red and gold hair was thick and long, enclosed with a headdress of purple and orange feathers. Her blue face had a strip of red over her eyes like a mask, but I knew that face too well. It was the twin sister of Yoona, and when she opened her mouth, she spoke with Yoona's voice.

'Angels . . . ?' she said.

She looked at me, then at Lis and the klopper. This Yoona's eyes flashed like red-orange steel and she jabbed her spear at us. She spoke, and her words held no more welcome that her cold-flashing eyes.

'Bad angels.'

8   Angels of death

She just stood there and glared at me. She had on a sleeveless
jacket of what looked like leather with iron strips across
the shoulders, knee-length leather pants and cross-strapped
sandals. A short sword was stuck in her belt and her mouth
was set in a grim, hard line.

'Where are the other angels?' she said. Her voice was
slow and she spoke with a heavy accent.

'We're all friends,' I said, taking a step forward.

Just one step, because she pushed hard and knocked me
back over the bed. Lis made to move and the spear-point
flashed at her.

Now, through the settling dust, other human figures were
coming in, all teenage and mix-coloured like her. Some
were blue and red, others green and brown, red and green,
blue and light-brown yellow. They were genetic mixes of
the Martian colonist groups, but the colours had slapped
everywhere as though out of a paintbox. A boy with red-
yellow hair in a mohawk came up behind the Yoona-one.
He had on the same leather jacket and leggings and was
brown-skinned with one red arm and green fingers and a
blue patch covering one eye and ear. I had to blink again,
because there was something familiar about him. Then he
scowled at me and I realised he was just about my twin.
The Yoona lookalike was about to speak again when behind
her, a girl with blue and brown stripes all over and a braid
of green hair, yelled and pointed. 'Klopper!'

The Yoona lookalike snapped something quickly and the

boy like me unslung his bow and fitted an arrow. 'No!' I yelled. 'You can't kill it.'

I stood up and so did Lis, blocking the klopper with our bodies. The boy was already pulling back his bow, but there was a sudden streak of yellow light across us and laser-fire splattered the metal walls. 'What's going on?' yelled a voice.

It was our Yoona, coming down the steps, followed by Gret and Bren. All three had lasers; they must have heard us and stopped to arm themselves before appearing. Yoona stopped and gaped as she saw her blue and red twin and the other one stared back, open-mouthed. Not so the others, who had strung arrows to bows, bolts to crossbows, and all of them pointed at us. They were more than twenty against our five, and if they all let go at once there would be a massacre. Yoona came down the steps, her rifle still raised, and stopped on the bottom stairs. I think she was going to tell them her name, but the other Yoona lookalike spoke first.

'You are Yoona-Angel.'

'And who are you?' said Yoona.

'Bala.' She indicated the tense, coloured faces behind her. 'Young ones of Araxes People, Solie Tribe.' She looked around us, pointing with her finger, knowing us all. 'Gret-Angel, Bren-Angel, Lis-Angel and Conn-Angel.' She paused, still looking. 'Where Reb-Angel, Zak-Angel and Cei-Angel?'

'Dead,' said Yoona.

'Bad angels. All should die,' muttered my lookalike beside her, and there was a murmur of agreement from the others, all the sharp arrows and bolts still pointed straight at us.

'Let us talk,' said Yoona quietly.

I don't know if they would have. But there was another of those sparkling flashes of static up the wall and the dancing light force appeared again. Deepwater shuddered and moaned and all the Solies jumped a little, maybe thinking they were in the belly of a giant beast.

'We talk outside,' said Bala, a little too quickly.

Yoona nodded. 'Outside,' she said.

Outside, the sky was an orangy colour with some orange-white clouds in it. It was cold, but none of the Solies seemed to feel it. The ground was broken into those huge jagged rocks, but the little green spike-bushes were everywhere. Deepwater's landing marks ploughed like a huge red furrow behind us.

As soon as she was out of the airlock, Yoona set her laser rifle on safety and lowered it. She motioned Gret and Bren to do the same, and after a moment they did so. 'We won't resolve this with fighting,' she said.

Maybe not, but some of them thought we could. The Conn lookalike for one – the others called him Hordo – still had his bow tightly strung and I knew that look on his face too well. He was waiting for a chance to use his arrow.

'How did you know we were coming?' said Yoona.

'Old, old legend,' said Bala. 'It tells us the spaceship will come with Martian life from the skies.'

'A gene drop,' said Yoona. 'But it didn't function.'

'Kloppers are there!' shouted a girl with spiked yellow hair, green down one half her body, blue and black the other. 'The enemy from long ago.'

There was a shout of agreement from the others. 'If we let you live, the kloppers must die,' said Bala and there was another shout, Hordo louder than anyone.

'One-colour angels,' he jeered.

'Better than looking like an explosion in a paint factory,' I growled and we looked at each other, each knowing we were going to fight very soon.

'Give us kloppers,' said Bala.

'They weren't put on Deepwater for you to destroy,' said Yoona. Her face was calm and her voice quiet, but they all shut up when she spoke. 'They're part of the Deepwater mission.'

Behind us, the spaceship groaned and some of that static played down the outside of the hull, making it shudder like a beached whale. There was tension now – some of the Solies were getting really scared and ready to panic.

'Stand aside!' yelled Bala.

'Or die with them,' shouted Hordo. 'We know what kloppers will do.'

'Why, did you ask them?' yelled another voice from behind them.

That was Lis. She was truly our Lis-Angel, because she was the angel of life that day for us and probably a lot of Solies. On the long run-in to landing, she'd actually started talking to the klopper leader and he was grateful we'd saved his life. So when all of us went out with the Solies, Lis-Angel unstrapped him and released the other kloppers from the NUN chamber. It was a big risk, but no worse than what the Solies wanted to do. Now they were ranged in a row behind her about thirty of the olive-green tanks, the klopper leader towering over Lis, spears and crossbows pointed.

'Let my friends go,' said Lis and the klopper leader nodded beside her.

Bala hesitated, a real scowl of anger on her face. But she had only about twenty Solies with lighter weapons than the massive crossbows the kloppers carried. There were mutters of rage and Bala gave a very Yoona-like glare as she lowered her spear. But of course my lookalike, Hordo, was too thick to see that. He was already pulling back his bowstring and raising it when I pushed him hard and we both went down in the red Martian dust. His arrow arched high over Deepwater and the kloppers raised their bows, growling. A shout from their leader stopped them.

Hordo and I rolled over, punching hard. From his first scowl, I knew we would end up fighting. He was just like me and I was *sick* of guys like him, so thick and stupid that all they can understand is violence. We rolled over,

78

thumping and punching, and round us nobody moved. He got me in the ribs and I jabbed him with a real boxer's punch right on his sneering mouth. He kicked clear, spilling his arrow quiver. He grabbed one, maybe to stick it in me. I grabbed for it too, and with a loud clunk-thud another arrow stuck in the ground between our hands. It was not just one of their light arrows either; this one was big and long with a heavy iron tip. I forgot about rearranging Hordo's face and sat up.

A new group of Solies had arrived. There were more than fifty of them, all armed, but only the man who fired had his bow raised and he slung it back on his shoulder. They were dressed like our group; some were teenage and some older, all patterned with that vivid splashing colour-mix. Everything went deadly quiet and one of them came forward. She was tall, her red skin patched with blue and with one green hand. Her hair was yellow and red and her eyes yellow-brown. She looked like Bala and it was like seeing Yoona, thirty years on.

'I am The Yohna.' She looked at our Yoona and smiled. It was a good smile. 'My title comes from your name, Yoona.'

Gret rolled her eyes and muttered and I nearly grinned as I scrambled to my feet. The Yohna was looking at us all now, then up at the assembled kloppers and beyond them to the massive bulk of Deepwater. She looked back at her daughter, at Hordo picking himself up and all the others. There was a little pattering sound as they dropped their bows and arrows.

'Forgive my daughter – she is young and scared,' The Yohna said. Bala met her mother's eyes but shuffled like a kid caught doing something wrong. 'Deepwater Angels, you are welcome here.'

They had bought food, a sort of fish stew with beans and lichen. It tasted really good, and they shared it with the kloppers. But four-clawed kloppers eating with their hands are even worse than me with spaghetti. Bala and her friends drew off, but Hordo kept giving me looks like he wanted to finish the fight.

All of us were really stunned. The Yohna and her party knew about us, but not in the same angry way. Even the kloppers sensed that, and their row of crossbows and spears drooped like dead flowers. Overshadowing us all, the bulk of the Deepwater spaceship still shuddered, and even groaned like a whale with a bad stomach pain.

'Your spaceship is fighting itself,' said The Yohna.

Our Yoona stepped forward. She put her hands on her hips and began to speak, and she was never more our commander than at this moment. She told what had happened from the very beginning, the first universe flight, then the second, the prexes, the danger. She spoke directly and simply and everywhere the Solies were silent, even among Bala's group. She bent her head forward, letting her long red and dark-blonde hair fall round her face. Even Hordo stopped fiddling with his bow. Yoona finished and her voice caught on the last words.

'But we still have our human gene bank on board. So we're not angels. We failed to put life back on planet Earth.'

'You have failed?' said The Yohna. 'Twice you made the longest and most dangerous voyage of all humans. You fought everything and won, sometimes without knowing why you fought.'

She looked round at her silent people, then up at the bulk of Deepwater again. She touched a little silver triangle around her neck. It was a voice disc and it once must have spoken the legends of Deepwater, but now it was long since silent and just the badge of her leadership. She touched it again and began talking.

'Let me tell you the story of our people.' Her voice flowed on like music.

Deepwater took off from Mars in the last decade of the

twenty-first century. By then Earth was a dead planet and a plague was striking down the last colonists. Ours and another Deepwater were launched and the survivors expected to die. But incredibly, some did not. Another group survived by gene-splicing with the kloppers and their descendants live in South Mars to this day. But the 'human' group broke away and trekked all the way across a hostile landscape to their old North Mars settlements. At first they had to use cloning to swell their numbers; they had the gene bank left over from the Deepwaters before babies were born again. That was why we could see familiar faces round us in the various family groups.

There were three intelligent life-groups on Mars now. These, the North Mars Solies, in the south the hybrid human-kloppers, and far away to the west, a Martian people, the Dromo, about which they knew almost nothing. Dromos evolved like kloppers as the first life-forms on Mars, brought back when the terraforming began, but they kept away from humans and human-kloppers. The Yohna said they were like tailless, intelligent, two-legged lizards.

And Mars was *not* a dead planet, so a gene drop would only have added the alien life to life already here. The air was thin and the gravity light, but everywhere was life, in the little scuttling things underfoot, the insect-birds and the bigger life like sand-tigers and ice-worms; also everywhere was the little spiked cacti, purple lichen, yellow and blue flowers and a gold-green creeper that seemed to stick out of the red rocks by itself.

The colonists had survived because they were tough and learned to live together. And because they had their legend passed on by word of mouth when the voice discs fell silent; that one day the Deepwaters would return and take them back to the shining star called Planet Earth, give them a richness and plenty they had never known on Mars.

'But over these many thousand years, we had learned to love our cold, hard planet,' said The Yohna softly.

So the Deepwater legend became black and terrible. The Deepwater Angels became demons who would take them from their known home to the unknown. And when the fix of stars and planets was right, as the legends foretold, when Deepwater appeared, the young ones headed by Bala and Hordo went out first to destroy it and keep their world safe from the bad Angels of Deepwater.

'We were right!' shouted a high voice. It was the girl with spiked yellow hair, green, blue and black down her body. She had a look of Gret in her face. 'They brought the kloppers to destroy us.'

For a moment we thought all the trouble and anger would spring up like one of those sand-tigers The Yohna talked about, but she sprang round, a hand up and her yellow-brown eyes on fire. 'Nothing can destroy us unless we *let* it!' she yelled.

'Nothing!' echoed her daughter, Bala, also jumping up, I think surprised by what her mother had said.

'What about us?' growled a voice.

It was the klopper leader. They'd all stood silent while The Yohna spoke, but now the crossbows and spears were lifting again and I couldn't blame them. They'd just heard they were a primitive life-form no longer existing, so their own planet was now a scary nightmare world.

I couldn't help myself, but I stepped forward; so, I think, did Bren and Lis. 'Yes, the kloppers have a right to live, it's *their* planet!' I yelled.

The Yohna swung round, a silencing hand towards her own people, stopping any words. Then she looked at me and it was like being hit by an invisible hammer. 'Yes. To the east there is room. They can go.'

She walked forward and raised her green hand. The klopper leader crunched forward and raised his clawed paw. They came together and I think that was the most important moment in all Mars history. 'We will give you guides to point the way.'

The klopper leader looked at her in his blank eye-slitted way, then at me and one green claw beckoned. 'Conn.'

I went up. The klopper lowered his voice, but it was still harsh, growling and loud in the thin Martian air. 'NUN told us what to do. These humans tell us what to do when we go east. Will someone else tell us what to do?'

They were afraid of being led, just like I was led with Reeboks and the fear of what would happen to Mum. I thought for a moment, then saw Reeboks' face, his finger pointed at Denie and his insults seemed to clang like a bell in the thin Martian air. I knew what to say.

'That's easy. Make your own lives and if anyone tells you to do something you don't like, just show them who's boss. Tell them no way!'

'Too easy . . . ?' frowned the klopper, blinking his big heavy green eyelids. But maybe what I was saying got to him, maybe he trusted me, because this thick wide mouth spread into as close to a smile as I had ever seen. 'No way! Is that all?'

'Yes, that's all.'

It made me think of my own Earth-life, of being power-less, stressed and looking for good times. Then I breathed more thin Martian air into my lungs and looked round, the dream broken. But there was silence and on the different-coloured faces was puzzlement, some frowning uncertainty but also some understanding. The Yohna was smiling, so was the bowman beside her, who had shot at me and Hordo. He was red and yellow-brown with a black arm, and his hair was in blue-green dreadlocks. But his face was Robbie grown up and, like The Yohna, he was smiling at me.

The kloppers understood straight away. Maybe having simple minds is good sometimes. They all turned and marched off into the red broken ground chanting 'No way! No way! No way!' like a music beat to their tramping feet. The leader turned once to raise his spear at me in farewell. I still didn't know his name.

The Yohna pointed her finger at four of the teenagers as guides. Her daughter Bala stepped forward, though, and the pointing green finger stayed on her with a little smile of approval. Hordo stepped forward, too, then glanced at me and half-raised his hand. I don't know if he was inviting me to another fight, but he did smile and the red dust clouds rose round him as he fell in behind the marching kloppers. Their 'No way! No way! No way!' refrain lingered after the orange-red clouds had settled round them. They would be scared of nothing.

We sat around for about an hour while the dust clouds settled again. Most of the people just looked at us shyly, in silence because we were out of their dreamtime and legends. Behind us, Deepwater lay still, static still playing along its length and making those small groaning noises. It cast a black shadow over the red ground and behind it stretched the long furrow made by its landing.

'Where will you go from here?' said The Yohna. There was something careful in the way she spoke, and how she looked at the Robbie lookalike beside her.

'Where can we go?' said our Yoona, sounding desperate. 'We have to somehow make the gene bank work and to do that we must get Deepwater back to Earth—' She stopped because a big hush came down over everyone as she said that. 'What is it?' she said.

'End of the Deepwater legend,' said The Yohna, and looked very sad.

The Reb-bowman beside her took it up, reciting words that were legend. 'And when the angels return, that will be the end of their mission and with life back in the solar system, that will be the end of the far-travelled Deepwater.'

'End?' whispered Yoona in the sudden stillness. '*What* end? We haven't ended, we—' She stopped, because through the high notes in her voice, an even higher sound screamed through the dust-laden air.

It was the sound of Deepwater itself and the spaceship shuddered, throwing itself sideways like a beached whale trying to breathe. A voice, neither male or female, but mixed loud and screaming like both, came howling from the sudden silence that followed.

'Warning! Warning! Deepwater's self-destruction will take place in one hour.'

Deepwater groaned again and a last burst of static crackled along its side. We all stood there, unable to believe what we'd heard, but it continued, repeating the same message in that loud screaming voice.

'Self-destruct in one hour. One hour!'

9 Where demons are

We stood there, while that voice echoed over the broken red landscape. It was COL's voice – even I knew that, and as it spoke all the static electricity flickered to a stop and Deepwater seemed to sink more deeply into the Martian sand.

'No . . . that can't happen,' breathed Yoona.

'Yes,' said The Yohna behind us, touching her disc again. 'This was the end of the legend. Angels return and Deepwater destroy.' She turned, clapping her hands, and the crowd began to move off. Some of the younger ones remained, looking at their legend for the last time as COL's voice echoed again over the broken red land.

'Fifty-six minutes.'

'Why?' yelled Bren.

Quickly, with that iron voice echoing the passing minutes, The Yohna told us why. The impact of Deepwater would be too great on any culture established on Mars, whether for good or bad. But even the best programming can't be perfect. Ours did not – could not – plan for a return to Mars with the Earth's human gene bank on board.

'We have to tell COL that,' yelled Gret. 'Tell it to stop.'

'COL's not responding,' said Yoona. 'It must be part of the programme.' She was right, the flat COL tones confirmed what she said, echoing again in the thin Martian air.

'Fifty-four minutes.'

'You can find shelter with us,' said The Yohna.

'No!' shouted Yoona back. 'We *must* deliver the human gene bank to Earth!'

'Yoona, it's too late,' said Bren. 'Too late,' echoed Gret and Lis, and COL's iron voice counted off the minutes, confirming this.

'Fifty-three minutes.'

'Not if we can get to COL,' I said.

'COL is sealed off – there's no way,' said Gret.

'There's always a way,' I yelled back. I didn't really know that, but the little static buzz was *telling* me there was.

Yoona took just one second to make up her mind. 'Gret, Bren, stay in the command deck until fifteen minutes before detonation. Then get out quick. Lis, take the gene bank clear. Connal, come on!'

She grabbed my hand, but I looked back at The Yohna for a moment. She smiled and lifted her green hand in a salute, in pride, and we all scrambled back into the sloping decks of Deepwater.

'We should wait for you,' yelled Lis.

'No, get clear, order, order!' yelled Yoona. Gret and Bren ran up the stairs, Gret spinning round for a moment in the upper hatchway. 'You'd better be right, you prexing Earthkid!' she yelled, unexpectedly grinning before she followed Bren.

Lis was already grabbing the gene bank and making for the port again. Yoona grabbed me again, hair tumbling around her face, eyes glaring like lasers. 'All right, Conn. You are the eighth casket and somehow all this is a challenge for *you* to meet – now *where* do we go?'

There was no static buzz under my tongue now, just me, my mouth shut and a million silly thoughts whirling through my mind. Yoona slammed me against the wall, yelling, 'You were put on Deepwater for a reason. *This* is the reason, now where do we go?'

What had the klopper leader said? The demons below. Something below, stopping and scaring them. If NUN cloned the kloppers then COL was their enemy. Did that mean COL was stopping them—

'*Where*, Conn?' Yoona screamed.

'Below,' I muttered.

Yoona flipped open the deck trap and we ran down the narrow steps leading to the flight bay, Deepwater's lower jaw. The Wingfish was there, but apart from that it was gleaming white, streamlined and empty. Yoona looked round.

'This is the only "below" we know about,' she gasped. 'If there's an entrance to the Martian gene bank, then it must be here.'

'Did COL or NUN ever say anything?' I said.

'No.'

Typical adults, I thought, always wanting the power. We looked round, Yoona at the walls and ceiling, me at the bottom because I was thinking about tunnels and tunnels start at ground level. 'Yoona, is that something?'

She looked down. Inset in the far wall, just behind the Wingfish, was the faint outline of something like a super-large mouse-hole. Yoona knelt beside it and looked up, yelling, 'COL, lower flight bay, what is this entrance behind the Wingfish?'

There was silence for a moment, then COL just said, 'Forty-five minutes.'

Yoona hammered on the door. 'There's no opening. It must be COL-controlled.'

'Let me try,' I said. One thing I can do well is kick. Ms Booth our teacher says she never wants to get in my way because I am a natural kicker, but just don't kick in the right direction, whatever that means. I still had on my metal-soled boots and I lined up and charged forward. It was like kicking a steel wall and I stepped back, kicking again. This time my toes seemed to drop off, but I kicked again. *This* time, something sparked like short-circuiting and the wall-hatch suddenly fell inward. The people who built Deepwater never planned for the force of a Connal-kick.

Yoona pushed it sideways and crawled in. I followed.

We could just stand up in the tunnel that opened before us like a gleaming metal tube. It stretched on down into darkness and I looked up. Overhead was a close-fitting round hatch the klopper must have come down. But he had seen demons.

Yoona set off down the tube and I followed, our footsteps clattering round us as we ran. For a second I felt that we were being scanned by something: COL went everywhere in this ship. As we ran, automatic lighting came on round us, pushing back the darkness. Suddenly we ran into a solid blackness that slammed us back.

Then the black forcefield door vanished and something rushed out, rearing up on short-legged feet, roaring at us from the distance of almost zero millimetres. It was fork-tailed and scaled green and yellow, with purple flaring eyes. It sprang at us again, but was pulled up short as though caught by an unseen chain. I could feel the blast of its hot breath against my face and had to step back.

'What is it?'

'Martian sand-tiger,' said Yoona.

The thing roared, lashing its tail again, and from the open mouth shot out a long red tongue. But something happened to the end of it, misting and flickering as though the tongue-tip disappeared.

The thing roared at us again, shooting out its red tongue and again, the tongue-tip seemed to slick and vanish. Now on the wall round us the electric lightning was beginning to crackle as though the static storm above was spreading through all Deepwater.

'What's happening to its tongue?' I shouted.

Yoona hesitated for a moment and then she walked straight at the thing. It gaped at her, snapping sharp curving blue teeth at her and they shut through her face. Yoona looked back with a pale grin. 'Solid-hologram behind a forcefield,' she said. 'Come on.'

Only Yoona would have stuck her head into the tiger's

mouth to find out. I took a deep breath and walked forward. The thing wasn't just a real hologram, it was super-real. We felt the hot-cold breath and walking into the creature was like walking into its insides. The eyes became eyeballs and brain, then we entered the body, a pumping red mass of lungs, heart and intestines. It was so real, warm and horrible that I choked, but Yoona's firm hand pulled me through. The forked tail flickered up into our faces and the hologram disappeared with a faint clicking into silence.

There was no sound now, as though the forcefield behind had sealed everything off. But the tunnel stretched on into darkness and we began to run, the heavy clatter of our boots sounding on the rounded corridor like metal handclapping. We ran and ran down the endless gleaming length and now there was no COL voice ticking off the minutes. We just ran and I kept thinking how crazy this was – we didn't even know if it would lead anywhere. But the sand-tiger hologram said something; it was put there to frighten people, people like kloppers who might wander round the insides of Deepwater. So there must be something ahead that they wanted hidden.

We kept running and running. A cool dark air was rushing past us and the gleaming soft lighting went on ahead. Another hologram thing like a primitive form of klopper-life sprang up, but I shut my eyes and barged through, not wanting to see its insides.

Now the tunnel seemed full of nightmares, as though something was throwing them up to make us stop. Suddenly a little flock of those trites whirled and swooped, jabbing their stings at me. Another flock of dark blue solid bullet-shaped insects, stonebugs they were called, then a writhing, snapping fanged mass of ice-worms, so real and horrible I could feel their slimy coils round me. Ahead, Yoona stopped and I crashed into her.

We had run into another black force-wall. This was solid. Yoona bashed it and kicked it, but the force just threw us back. Yoona looked up and pointed, yelling loudly. 'Overhead!'

There was a hatch there I couldn't see. I made my hands into a cup and boosted Yoona up. She punched open another hatch and swung herself up, reaching down to grab me. Yoona was strong and pulled me up easily.

Inside was a ladder leading up. Yoona paused and looked at me. 'This might lead nowhere,' she said. 'It's a hell of a chance.'

'We have to take a hell of a chance,' I said.

She nodded and we began to climb, my boots slipping on the smooth ladder-rungs. Sometimes Yoona's boots trod on my hands and it seemed we were climbing as long as we were running. Then suddenly the steel funnel swayed and Yoona stopped, her boots treading on my fingers again as a hot sweaty blast of air hit us then drew back and blew forward again, like breathing.

'Something wrong with the metal,' she said.

It seemed to be stretching somehow, smoothing and rippling out as we held on to the rungs. Then it suddenly looped forward and became a tunnel again, as though the metal was so close to an intense powerful force that it was melting. The surfaces were even bleeding large blobs of jelly when suddenly we were thrown forward into a wide room, like no room I had ever seen before.

This room seemed to ripple and move like heartbeats. It pulsed and quivered, seeming to be shot through with dazzling little stars of red light; everywhere hung glowing blue-gold balls of fire. Some were at ground level, some up in the air and all of them linked by straight laser-lines of light, like patterns on a computer; they went hexagonal, round, square, twining into each other and making different shapes, never stopping. It was electronics, but in a strange way more than that, as though all of it made up the living force of a human body. Then suddenly, chilling us, sounding close, COL's voice came back on-line.

'Eight minutes.'

'COL!' yelled Yoona. I was expecting her voice to echo, but it didn't; somehow it was soaked up in the darkness around. Some of the light patterns swirled a little, making the blue-gold fire-balls move closer to each other.

'COL, I *command* you to answer!'

There was a long pause before another voice came, like COL's but in a funny way different. It was a voice I had heard before from somewhere a long way away. 'Deepwater's flight program is ended, Yoona. You must leave. I will delay the countdown until you are clear.'

'We can't leave,' Yoona screamed, making the light forces swirl again. 'Deepwater's mission is not complete!'

'I cannot alter primary programming.' The voice filtered back into that light and dark stream like different-coloured waters flowing together. 'Leave Deepwater.'

'No! We are breaking your programme!'

'The human race will survive on Mars, perhaps one day return to Earth.' Now that light voice held an incredible note of sadness and I knew it – *knew it*! It was Chibbi's voice – she was the spirit force of this electronic heart. Yoona knew it, too, and she looked at me then forward into the light forces.

'You must. We will change your programme!' she said.

'No!'

There was something else in the voice now – a note of fear. All the blue fire-balls came together and a strong black wind blew at us, making us stagger back. A forcefield was forming, sealing COL from us, and Yoona sensed it at the same time. She staggered, her long hair blowing round her face and screamed into the wind. 'We must. We can!'

The black wind blew like a tempest, but Yoona put her head down, her hands out as though pushing an invisible iron barrier aside. She walked forward and I tried to follow, but was pushed back. Only Yoona could pass through that forcefield and suddenly she was standing in the blue cone of light-fire and it streamed up round her. A blast of energy threw me off my feet and crashed through my body with a cold-flame intensity. It beat and whirled round us both and from somewhere came the COL-voice with that same echo of Chibbi, an echo of sadness and fear.

'Programme broken.'

Everything went still. The cold little fire lights still twinkled, but somehow all the power force had drained away. Yoona was on her knees, her head forward and I went over. Her eyes were shut, but she was still breathing and I helped her stand, looking round.

'Why, COL?' I asked. 'Why were you scared? Why sad?'

There was no answer, but inside me something whispered as though from a huge distance that understanding would come. That whisper was touched with sadness and fear, too, and I turned and walked out of the force-room. I had to carry Yoona now. I was going back, not the way I came but another, down a narrow path with giant power rings on either side that were the energy power of the Deepwater engines. They shone like huge white circles cut in the blackness, but I just kept walking, aware of the cold jelly-feeling of another forcefield round me, one that went solid underfoot like ice freezing.

Black ice. We were back in the room that, months ago it seemed, Yoona had told me led to COL. I knew where I was now and the crystal door opening to the NUN chamber swung gently out. That huge football pitch room where we had all woken up was silent, but the grey walls seemed a different colour. Carrying Yoona, I passed the caskets and went on to the other end.

I was tired and aching, but it didn't matter. I was ready to collapse, but I knew I would keep going. I went down the long corridor to the below deck, Yoona feeling lighter and more limp now.

The Yohna, the Martian leader, was waiting there. With her was the Reb-bowman, Lis, Gret and Bren. They looked

94

at me as though I was back from the dead. I didn't find out until later that COL's 'Programme broken' had rung like a death-scream through the ship with a last fusing blast of static.

'You have control of Deepwater now,' said The Yohna. 'You have a long journey.'

My head spun. Bren and Lis were trying to help me, but I put Yoona on the bunk myself. A long journey, yes; I had my fifth prex coming, and Yoona had said the fifth one was always the worst. Yoona was now lying still and quiet on her bed, her eyes shut, the commander of Deepwater who had given everything for her mission, who used her own life-force to fuse and stop the power of COL like two flames meeting. I knew she was dead – we all did.

'A long journey,' repeated the Yoona lookalike.

She was looking at me and her headband sparkled. The sparkle became a slow spinning streak of flame and she was saying something else, but I couldn't hear it. I felt my head bang against the wall and the room spun sickeningly to throw me back across time and space into the unknown of my last prex.

10   To the mountain top

'That's the second time you've done that, Connal,' said Mum.

'What, Mum?'

I sat up, blankets round my legs. I was still on the couch, so I must have slept there last night – Earth-sleep through everything happening on Deepwater – and my neck was a bit sore. I rubbed it and looked out of the window. It was morning again.

'You just flaked out,' she said. 'I had to leave you on the couch. You're too heavy to pick up.' She rubbed her eyes and went into the kitchen to make some coffee. Mum is always tired.

I rubbed my neck again. There was already that horrible feeling of distance from Deepwater, and at the very worst time. Yoona was gone – I couldn't bring myself to say 'dead' yet – and that only left Bren, Gret and Lis to fly Deepwater back to Earth. It left all sorts of terrible unknowns happening in the spaceship while I was back here on Earth, thinking about new realities, just as important. Mum came back with the coffee.

'That insurance reward's going to make a difference,' she said.

I sat up straight. All the fears of what Reeboks spelled out came rolling over me. We were associated with Roger and the bank might cut us off. 'Will it pay the mortgage?' I asked.

'It'll make a dent in it,' said Mum. 'Better if the payment was more than half, but—'

'Who got the other half?' I yelled. 'I did all the hard work.'

'I don't know,' said Mum. 'Somebody who helped with information, I suppose. What do you want for breakfast?'

'I don't want any breakfast, Mum,' I said. 'I've got things to do.'

'What things?' she called, but I was already heading out of the door to my bike.

All the pieces were falling into place like a big easy jigsaw. There was only one person who could have scored half the reward for information and I knew who the little rat was. And I was raging for another reason, because once again I was torn away from the reality of Deepwater and Mars and back on Earth, fighting a battle I had really fought thousands of years before. Because I knew now that I was from Deepwater, not Earth – even the houses whizzing by had a funny cardboard look to them. But the anger in me was real, as real as Deepwater, Mars and even the purple lichen over red rocks. As real as Yoona's death, saving her spaceship.

Reeboks lived in a much better street than me. Nobody in this street would have been caught dead in Mum's little dairy, for they shopped at fancy delis and shopping centres. Reeboks' house was at the end; there was a garage under the house and the big swing door was open. It was still early and his dad's car was inside, not second-hand like my Mum's but one of those big classy jobs. I got off my bike, still angry but careful because Reeboks' dad appeared, about to get into the car. Mr Wilson looked over at me, tossing his briefcase into the back.

'Graeme's gone out,' he said.

'OK, then, I'll talk to you.'

Just a day ago, I wouldn't have gone within a mile of Mr Wilson. But now I was still feeling that anger and a power-charge as though Reeboks, his dad and the bank didn't matter.

'Don't you dare cancel my mum's mortgage because she had some trouble with the cops.'

'What?' he said.

'It wasn't Mum's fault, it was mine, the cops will tell you that!'

Mr Wilson just looked at me. He was a sort of tall, bald version of Graeme, in a neat grey suit and with steel-rimmed glasses. So I told him, shouting, as quick as I could and finished, 'So there's no way you can take it off Mum.'

He just sat there listening. He didn't explode or pull rank the way I thought he would. He just shrugged, thought for a moment and then said 'Kid, I'm not working for the bank any more. I was made redundant when our bank merged with another.'

I remembered Reeboks talking about the merger. 'I . . . I thought you were going to be one of the top guys in it,' I said.

'So did I,' he said, and shrugged again. 'I still leave the house at this time and come back in the afternoon.' He paused. 'I haven't told my wife and Graeme yet, as I was hoping to land another job first.' He looked at me, not sure I think, why he was saying all this. 'Kid, for what it's worth, all any bank cares about is repayment on time. If Graeme said anything else, he was making it up.' He sighed. 'The way I've been making it up for the last week.'

I didn't know what to say. I could've told him to tell his wife, but he knew that and couldn't, not yet. It was his problem and too personal for me to talk about.

'I hope you get a new job,' I said.

He just nodded, got into the car and went off. I backed my bike over the other side of the street, leaned on the handlebars and waited. The sun was hot, my head spun and I found myself wishing that I could prex back to Deepwater – then, shaking my head, knowing it was too soon, that there was still too much to do.

Reeboks showed up about ten. He wheeled his bike into the garage, whistling, sticking his legs out and really showing off. I followed him in and he didn't hear me – or see me until he turned. Then he jumped, his eyes went wide and he clutched at a parcel he was holding.

'Spending it already, Graeme?'

'Who told you—' he began. Then he shut his mouth, but that was enough for me and I wasn't scared of Reeboks any more or scared of his power. I wasn't insecure any more either, and was too strong now to even feel angry.

'Connal, let me—'

'No!' I shouted.

He yelled even louder. 'Yeah, Connal, I took half the insurance, we're winners, Connal, that's what winners do, they go for it. But I did it for you, Connal.' Reeboks hunched himself down behind his handlebars and blinked his eyes wide, waiting for me to reply.

I felt something creepy come over me as though I was waiting for Reeboks to say that. 'For me, Reeboks?'

'Yes, Connal.' Now his voice was part of the creepy-feeling and I had heard it before, across time and space on Deepwater. His eyes flashed for a moment. 'I've been into town and I've bought you lots of stuff, CDs and that new gear for your computer.' His eyes flashed again. 'We're still mates, aren't we, Connal?'

No, we weren't still mates. Reeboks had gone out and bought that stuff in case I keyed in to what he did; in case I needed to be bribed. He still thought he could buy me. He still thought that money and power made the difference and using people was OK so long as everything turned out all right for him. I could hear my voice and it echoed as though across the endless blackness between Earth and Deepwater prexes.

'Keep it, Graeme. Just don't come near me again. You're not a friend, you're a lowlife. I don't need you.'

Reeboks sat there across his bike, his mouth open and a strange look in his eyes as though he didn't recognise me. Somehow his image flickered as though he was an image stuck on paper. I turned and cycled away. It was late morning, but I was getting a cold feeling like darkness over my body.

I didn't go home. I cycled around, sat down by myself then cycled again. I felt like a little piece of wood caught in a rushing river. So I kept cycling, everything rushing round me, wanting to go back to Deepwater but knowing there was no way to force the prex. Time and distance just slipped past as I cycled home, knowing I was finished with Reeboks, knowing the sky was growing darker because it was nearly night again. Like a rushing river, the day had slipped by me. And going home was cold, too, as though I was cycling into another darkness.

At home, I got another shock. Mrs Rasmussen was in the shop and through in the house, Chibbi and Denie were talking to Mum. They had drinks, crisps and were laughing together like they were getting on great. Chibbi was strumming her ukelele and waved at me.

'Connal, I'm off tomorrow. Thought I'd leave you a present. I want someone special to have it.'

She handed me the ukelele and I just gaped at her the way Reeboks did at me. 'Hey, but you've been round the world with this . . .'

'It's just a possession, Connal. I want someone special to have it.'

The bell dinged and Mum went into the shop. Denie muttered something about the bathroom and left too. I think that was arranged because Chibbi grabbed my shoulders hard and looked at me. 'Now listen, Connal. I know you think a lot of your dad. But it's your mum who held you together and kept things going. If you want to be a warrior, support her. That's a better act than all the movie tough-guys put together. *Comprendez*?'

That meant 'understand' in Spanish. I nodded and Chibbi's brown eyes went like searchlights again into mine. Outside it was dark now and I felt the cold presence of coming evil.

'Mars,' I said.

Chibbi put a gentle finger on my lips. 'No. Don't tell me. Just handle it. I know you can.'

And she wasn't putting me off, just power-charging more energy into me. Chibbi gave me her wonderful grin and a little kiss, just as Mum yelled to Mrs Rasmussen to close up the shop. Denie came out of the bathroom and all three smiled at each other as though sharing secrets. I sat there scowling a bit, but rather pleased they were taking this trouble over me. Anyway, I always scowl a bit.

'Did you tell him?' Mum asked Chibbi.

Chibbi shook her head. 'That's your job,' she said.

I just looked at them, keeping my strong scowl in place. Mum's lips trembled, but she smiled and suddenly looked younger. 'Connal, we're using some of the reward money to go back where Dad and I came from. We were both Irish and he was half-Polynesian from Rarotonga. We're going to both places and you can decide where you want to come from.'

'Both countries have mountains. You can climb them,' said Chibbi.

'Mum, you don't have to do this,' I said.

'Yes I do.' She pulled a parcel up from behind the sofa. 'And this is for you. I know you always wanted a pair.'

I only had to look at the label on the box. Reeboks!

'Connal, you're going to have the classiest feet in school,' grinned Denie.

I strummed the ukelele a little, then began to laugh. All the nightmare, all the coming sense of evil, fell away and it was suddenly so funny that all I could do was laugh and laugh. Then with a crash and horrible splintering of glass, the whole world seemed to come apart with an engine-roar and screech of brakes over grinding glass. And over that came a higher taunting yell from Roger. 'How do you like *this* ramraid, kiddo?'

He had driven his wagon right through the front window

of our shop, smashing the glass and everything else, and Mrs Rasmussen took a dive into the bread rack. He reversed, the glass scrunching under his wheels, his face a pale snarling mask behind the windscreen. He backed out, and we heard a crash as he hit another car across the road before he turned the vehicle to roar away out of sight. But the engine caught for a moment and I was already running, filled with more deadly rage that I'd ever known, through the shop with Mum yelling for me to stop. The glass scrunched under me as I leapt out of the window and over to the wagon.

Roger was trying to restart it. I flung open the door and grabbed at him. He kicked at me, but I hung on to his legs. I'm big and strong, but so was Roger and he snarled. 'You're going to need that insurance money to patch up your tinpot little shop!'

I gave an extra hard pull and he tumbled out over on top of me, landing a punch as he did. I whacked him back hard, one for Mum. 'My dad wouldn't know rats like you,' I yelled.

Denie must have charged right after me. She grabbed Roger's other leg and he was pulled further out. 'So who the hell cares what you think?' he yelled, and raised his fists to hammer me and Denie, then went a bit cross-eyed as Chibbi slammed the ukelele on his head. It only slowed him down for a moment, but that was long enough for Mum to come up and it was really bad luck for Roger because she had been baking pies.

Mum sold her pies in the shop. She used a rolling-pin for the pastry and it was on the kitchen bench when Roger crashed through. So when Denie grabbed Roger and Chibbi broke my ukelele over his head, Mum took just a moment longer to land the rolling-pin on him. I would never want Mum to hit me with anything, let alone a rolling-pin. Roger went even more cross-eyed and crashed forward on to Denie and me. With a great high howl, two cop cars came round the corner, red lights flashing, Roger still quiet among all the broken red-flashing glass. He didn't wake up until they handcuffed him.

'Sorry about your present,' said Chibbi.

Her ukelele was just bits of string and wood. The cops had taken Roger away and Mum was calling some people to patch our window. She and Denie were about to go. They were both smiling at me and, like Reeboks, they seemed to go flat for a moment like paper cut-outs.

'Robbie says you should try for the hockey team,' Denie was saying. 'Why don't we talk about it with him? Tomorrow?'

'OK, tomorrow.' My voice seemed to echo as I said that. For a strange moment I didn't know what tomorrow was. But I knew Denie was dead on Deepwater in her crystal casket. And Zak and Robbie and Yoona . . .

'Connal?'

Denie had gone over to the car and Chibbi was facing me alone. Her wonderful brown eyes shone in the lamplight and she held my arm tightly.

'You be a warrior,' she said. 'Everything will come right if you think straight. All the answers are there, right in front of you – they always have been. Just be strong enough to grab them.' Her voice was echoing from across time and space but on Deepwater, Yoona and I had broken the COL programme. 'Understand?'

'Yes, Chibbi.'

'*Adios*, my warrior Conn. We'll keep in touch.'

'Sure, Chibbi.'

I blinked because my eyes were misty. I blinked several times and when I had them open again, she was over at her little car, getting in. A hand waved out of the window as it drove off. My legs felt heavy now, as though I was walking like a puppet with strings tied to me. I went over to my bike and Mum called.

'Connal?'

'I'm just going for a quick ride, Mum,' I said.

She came up. I'd never noticed before, but my Mum has a really nice face. She pointed back at the shop. 'All this is going to cost a bit.'

I knew what she was saying and made myself smile, although everything spun again. 'I know Mum. It doesn't matter about the mountains in Ireland or Rarotonga.'

'It matters, Connal,' she said. 'We'll get there. Don't be late.'

My eyes were going misty again so I just nodded and biked off into the night. I felt warm and power-charged until something chill came over me again with a little screech of brakes as Reeboks swung in beside me. He was glaring, his hair slicked back by the wind, pedalling madly to keep up with me.

'My dad can fix all that!' he yelled. 'The bank will give you a loan! Connal, I can arrange all that, I can do it!'

I broadsided my bike and nearly knocked him over. 'Even if you could, I don't care any more! Understand – I don't care!'

'You can't do this! he yelled, his voice screeching like his brakes, then echoing into empty blackness. 'You need me, Connal!'

I kept on going and Reeboks didn't try to follow. He yelled behind me and I looked back once to see him under the yellow street light, eyes glaring and his shadow black round him, then kept going.

Reeboks didn't matter. Nothing mattered except pedalling hard up the hill and moonlight splashing the sea with silver. All this was new, too, a wonderful way of expressing myself, power-charging through me. At the top of the hill I could stop my bike, lift my hands to the black sky and stars and shout as loud as I could, because nobody would ever hear me.

'I know where I belong! I know where I belong!'

The stars spun and the whole dark world came round me and I gripped my handlebars, knowing the future was there and waiting for the spinning blackness to become a whirlpool, drawing me back across the dark endless nothing to Deepwater, to something that I knew now must happen.

The last battle of the human race.

11   The face of power

I was strapped to one of the beds in Deepwater's below deck, and alone; that's to say there was no one living there, because Yoona's body lay on the bunk beside me. I unstrapped myself, feeling sick, feeling as though my insides were being squeezed tight. They had covered her with a strip of some silvery stuff, but it was horrible looking at her like that. I pulled it off. She looked like a sleeping person, but her hands were cold to the touch and her hair was across her face.

I could feel tears coming. I've always hated tears, thinking they were weak, but these tears were strong, full of rage and sorrow. I didn't hear Lis come down the stairs and didn't know she was there until she gently put an arm round my shoulder. She sat with me for a few minutes, not saying anything, then we went upstairs.

The command deck had that same still horrible hush, like the memorial service I went to for my father. We were back in outer space and Mars was an orange dot in the distance. Gret was in Yoona's seat and Bren was beside her. Gret looked at me and smiled tightly. 'Listen,' she said and placed her hand on the console. 'COL, report status.'

'Twenty thousand kilometres from Mars, course set for Earth.'

We had COL back under control, so at least Yoona hadn't died for nothing. There was something strange, though, in the voice and Bren nodded as he saw my expression.

'Sounds like a very tired COL,' he said. He looked at

Gret, pressed his lips tight and said, 'Listen, Conn, what you did with Yoona saved us. Sorry we ever thought you weren't part of this crew.' It took a lot to say that, because Bren was as proud as me. But he even managed a grin and put out his hand. So did Gret and I grabbed them both, red and green, and we all smiled. Lis was less formal – she just hugged me tight from behind and it was the best moment, even with all our sadness, because I knew *this* was where I belonged.

The food machines were still working, so we had some blue biscuits and water and ate in silence. Outside was the starlit blackness of deep space and Mars was an even smaller orange-red behind us. It was strange to think of the humans we were leaving behind, there for thousands of years and now Martian, all different colours but the same. And some of them still in our image.

'There was a really nice blue and red Gret lookalike,' said Lis innocently. 'The one with yellow and brown hair who you kept looking at Bren, remember?' If Bren did remember, he didn't say anything, and even though he was already red-brown, I think he went a deeper red. Gret's look at him was pure green, though. But it was only a small joke and sad, because it reminded us of The Yohna and our Yoona below. Lis looked at me again. 'Conn, do you want to hear what we've worked out?'

'Sure.' I knew parts of it, but they'd been on Deepwater long enough to put most of it together. And the little static-buzz went under my tongue as Lis spoke, as though telling me we were locked into the truth.

'COL had a programme,' she said, 'to restore Earth-life as priority, then restore Martian-life if possible. But COL was given a choice because they – the people who programmed the flights – were not sure it would be needed.'

'COL's choice,' I said, 'was whether to drop the Martian gene bank or not. But whatever, Deepwater was to self-destruct because if it stayed alive' – that was a strange word, but it fitted – 'it would be too strong, have too much impact . . .' And be too powerful, said my static-buzzing thoughts.

'We overrode COL's programme,' said Gret. She pulled a hand hard down her green hair. 'The Deepwater programmers must have allowed for that, too, otherwise COL wouldn't be back on-line.'

'They must have—' I said, then stopped because the static-buzz became a flooding roar in my head, drowning my thoughts with such fantastic ideas that I had to shut my eyes, shut my mouth, just to let the incredible truth flood as loudly as it did. 'Evil never dies,' Chibbi had said and she was right; her words spoke loudly in my mind. Evil never died, but neither did good and there was a chance, just a tiny incredible chance, for all of us. Through that flooding static roar, I heard my voice speaking.

'I want to take Yoona to her casket.'

'We're going to do it soon,' said Gret softly, but looking at me very curiously.

'Now, please.'

Gret looked at Bren, then nodded. 'All right.'

I thought my tears were going to start again. They didn't, but I couldn't look at anyone as I went below. Gret and Lis followed, leaving Bren in control. I picked Yoona up from her bunk. She seemed very light for such a strong young woman and I walked back down the long corridor, Gret and Lis behind me, our shadows dragging in the flickering lighting. And a hundred million thoughts of time and space swirled together and made Yoona's body more heavy. The NUN door was ahead; Lis put her blue hand on the symbols of earth, fire and water, and the door swung open.

It was different! That little golden shimmer I had seen before was now pure bright yellow and dazzling, as though gold was buttered over everything. The golden light spread a rich glossy carpet underfoot, like the lichen I had seen on Mars, spotting and bubbling like a golden hot soup. Golden clouds hung overhead and golden shafts of light shot through the yellow mist like sunlight into a yellow ocean.

'What . . . ?' I heard Gret gasp behind me as the NUN door swung shut behind us.

'NUN is regenerated,' I said.

And we were in NUN's power. There was nothing to do but walk forward into this huge chamber of gold light and over to the caskets, all twinkling in dazzling yellow light points. Then, as though the sun had come from behind clouds, another strong light descended, so thick and powerful that it seemed to shimmer golden raindrops off our bodies. Beside me, Lis and Gret stood like statues, the golden pressing rainstorm enclosing them with yellow fire. Yoona's body was so heavy that I had to kneel and gently place it on the ground. Then I looked up into that golden intense dazzle, knowing Lis and Gret could not help, knowing this was my fight.

'NUN,' I said. 'You won. We broke COL's programme and made COL too weak to resist you. You are speaking with COL's voice, you will take Deepwater back to Earth, dominate the planet and be its life-force.'

Overhead, among the thick yellow rain-clouds, a voice spoke, as solid as pouring golden water. 'How do you know these truths, Conn?'

NUN knew how I knew, but was asking me anyway. I felt hot and melting, filled with that rich gold, heavy and unable to move.

'Your programming,' I muttered.

'My programming?' echoed the voice.

'Programmed to reactivate if Deepwater returns to Mars. But your makers did not realise how your nature would change. So COL fought you, but wore itself out keeping the balance.' All those light spots, the static, were the forcefields of the two computers meeting in battle.

'And now I am in control,' said that beautiful golden voice. Round us, the chamber shimmered even more in

110

soothing golden light, so unlike the dark fire-cold of COL below. 'You made it possible, Conn.' And Yoona's sacrifice, said my confused heavy thoughts.

'You weren't meant to,' I muttered. 'Came here for another reason . . .'

'Another reason,' echoed the mocking voice.

'Bring Yoona back to life,' I said, 'She's not dead yet, so you can do it.' The light blazed again, while beside me Gret and Lis stood with their heads bowed, helpless.

'How do you these things, Conn?' said the voice, still full of control. 'You know because it is programmed into you, into your prex.'

'Prex is only a gene memory,' I muttered, still not looking up. 'Nothing else.'

'Nothing else?' Again that controlled, mocking echo. 'Not just the memory. Computer-enhanced, graphically-stimulated into a back-up so that if all else failed, you would know where you came from . . .' the golden voice paused ' . . . and in that past life, find clues to this one. Did you find those clues, Conn?'

'No.' But I meant to say yes. Something static-buzzed and held my tongue. 'You always wanted control. The trites in deep space, you mutated them out of the Martian gene bank to try and control us. They only existed because of you. But you couldn't come into our prex.'

'No?' NUN's voice was a solid mocking golden wave, hammering at me. 'I *was* there, because my own NUN maker came from a gene cell cloned from your time.'

My time . . . my time . . . the golden mist thickened and for a moment NUN's voice changed to an echo of a voice I knew and I heard bike wheels in the NUN chamber behind me. Then, with a creeping unreal sense of evil, came a voice.

'Hi, Connal. I was always in your prex.'

Reeboks circled round me on his bike, his eyes flashing golden, his mouth set in that jeering smile. He was even chewing gum. 'I controlled you like I hassled Robbie and

Denie.' He circled again. 'I pushed you, Connal, and made you what you are.'

And it was horrible because as Reeboks looked at me, he was shifting and changing, growing into a man, blurring into another man, then another. I was seeing the three generations from Graeme Wilson, the boy who grew up to be a computer designer, the son who carried his work into the bio-field in the dark twenty-first century and the grandson on Mars who was called NUN and designed the second of Deepwater's massive bio-computers – who put his own controlling genius into his NUN computer because he wanted to dominate and live in the new world that would be made.

The NUN man sat on the bike and looked at me, a solid-hologram, I knew, but the most real I had seen. The bike-hologram faded and he stood there, tall and bald, with a thin face, dressed in a long silver track suit, a brown-skinned South Martian like Yoona but with the same eye-glitter as the kid I knew. There was a black star-mark high on one cheek like a scar that seemed to turn the corner of his eye up.

NUN, the man. I was looking at him.

'I could never be destroyed, Connal. I could be hurt, stopped but never destroyed and when you broke COL, I became all-powerful.' His thin, sharp smile seemed to fill the chamber with evil flashing teeth. 'Immortal. Because I will grow my own gene, programmed with all memories.' Now his smile flashed sharper teeth like dazzling razor gold. 'The lord of Planet Earth. The human race will live through me.'

'A lord . . .' My words choked. 'COL fought you. I threw Reeboks off – he didn't control me.'

There was just the slightest pause before the gold voice flooded back. The brown-gold man just grinned at me, seeming to grow taller in the drifting golden mist. 'No, Connal, you are mine because I can give you the thing you need most.'

'Life for Yoona . . .' I heard myself say 'Life for Zak, Reb and . . .' and someone else whose name was the most important, but I couldn't remember it through all this pressing golden light.

'More than that, Connal. The life you want most. Give me your total love and I will give you that life.'

What life was NUN talking about? I had to fight this, I *knew* this, I had to think about things that mattered. Like my mother, like my father, his denims and his big white sombrero, his voice on my tapes. I shut my eyes, then opened them again as something dropped in front of me – something that could not really exist.

It was a big white sombrero with a rattlesnake hatband and long feather. NUN's voice flowed round it, as thick as golden treacle. 'I can make your father. I have your gene and his. I can give you the thing you want most. Your father.'

My father. All the times I had sat in my bedroom, wanting to hear his bootsteps coming down the hall and my door being opened. Him sitting on my bed, playing his guitar, me not wanting to sleep but my eyelids getting too heavy to stay awake . . . I was listening to those bootsteps now, coming up the NUN chamber behind me. And a hand was coming down on my shoulder with a ring of silver and blue sparkling painfully into my eyes. And a voice, not scratchy and distant on an old cassette, but full, strong and living.

'Conny-boy?'

That was Dad speaking, so real it stabbed right through me, filling my body with a painful joy. It was my father's voice and I knew that if I looked up, I would see my father's face. And NUN would make my father and we would live our lost years. But Yoona was at my feet. I tried to look at her, but she was just a flat image, glued on the flatness of nothing.

'Connal?'

The voice behind me was puzzled, but still strong. All I had to do was turn my head and look up into my father's face. And when I did that, I could forget about Deepwater, Earth and Mars and lose myself in memory. I wanted to be wrapped in a golden NUN dream forever with my father. We could go anywhere and live any reality we wanted. My father's voice was impatient now and sad, and his hand tightened on my shoulder to turn me round.

'Connal, look at me.'

12 NUN truth

'No!' I yelled and jerked away. I don't know why I did. There was just an incredible feeling that I had to, that I must tear myself loose from things that did not really exist. Things that would make me like them, also not existing.

'I haven't got a father. My father is dead!' I could hear my own voice yelling with strength I never thought I had. My voice was ringing through the NUN chamber and I kept yelling, 'I've just got me and my friends and we're going to make this work!' I stood up, feeling the hand-clasp torn away, walking out of darkness and shouting up into the golden fire-burning light. 'You don't belong here.'

'No!'

The light beat in waves like an angry voice with just an echo of Roger denying he was a crook. It lasered through me, but I kept looking up and even in that moment I felt it become less strong. And in the golden voice, there sounded a tiny uncertain note.

'Not belong, Conn?'

'No, you don't belong. You should be dead,' I shouted. Then I thought about Roger again. 'You helped us once, but you can't help us now. We owe you nothing.'

The overhead floodlight swelled to a more intense heat, hotter and hotter as though NUN was becoming more and more steamed with anger and I stepped over Yoona's limp body, looking up for the first time. The sharp golden light dazzled my eyes, which watered in a stream down my cheeks as the golden light exploded sharply in my brain. Stronger

115

and stronger it burned, wavebeats of noise, just a faraway echo in them of Reeboks denying he was not my friend and I felt myself fall because it was too hot to stand up. I had no voice, because it was burned away, but from somewhere I could hear a loud Connal-voice.

'No! I don't care who you can make for me. I don't care what it costs. You just want things for yourself and we don't need you.'

'Need you, Conn,' said the voice, burning with a desperate golden fire.

'Don't need you,' I repeated and in a stunning flash, more blinding than all the golden NUN glare, I knew why.

I was programmed for this. The people who programmed Deepwater also programmed me, the kid from the eighth casket, last to come out but the most powerful kid in the universe. With the golden light streaming round me, I knew I had the secrets of life. I could stop NUN.

Just knowing that made me relax. In fact all this was faintly silly; I was just a suburban kid with problems. But we all have problems, said the silver thought-music, and it became more intense as it opened out all the paths I could follow.

A dream world like the world I lived in with Mum and Roger. Dream world like the storm-drain or a dream world living with my dad, my mum, making up our own lives as we went along, living whatever dream we wanted.

'Dream world?' I asked aloud.

There was just the slightest hesitation in the music as though realising it had said the wrong thing. It was my choice – the whole fate of the universe programmed into *my* awareness, and for me to decide. The silver thought-music in my mind was NUN, soothing me; I knew that and didn't mind, shutting my eyes as the golden voice spoke again.

'Dream world, Conn.'

Yes, dream world. My lips nearly formed the words, but

116

Chibbi's goodbye flashed sharply across my mind. 'My warrior Conn!' she had said and I remembered Robbie and Denie who would never wake up. They would have fought like this for me.

'NUN, destruct,' I shouted into the streaming golden silence, then again because I was angry at myself as well as NUN. 'Destruct – destruct!'

I don't know what I expected. The NUN chamber didn't open in a splitting explosion and just for a moment, the golden light blazed so strongly that my bones seemed to melt. Then it lessened and I stood there tottering, wondering if I had said the right thing; then the NUN light was fading, becoming thinner and more pale and NUN spoke with an effort that must have cost it even more energy, because the light went paler still.

'Need you, Connal.'

'We don't need you, NUN,' I shouted back and felt very bad because I knew NUN was dying. I saw the NUN figure again, just a flicker, then Reeboks on his bike with a pleading look before vanishing; his shoes were last to fade. With just a word I could have restored the programme and bought them back, but that was wrong – wrong because Yoona, Robbie and Denie had died. I knelt beside Yoona, put my hands on her blonde head and repeated the same words.

'Don't need you, NUN. Destruct. Destruct.'

I shouted that. I had to. NUN had lived too long and forgotten why it was created, so I looked up and shouted into the still-thick puddles of golden closeness that still floated round like spilled water. Then there was nothing, not even silence. A computer note sounded across everything and the golden light began to fade.

NUN died quietly, fading with a sigh. It was horrible listening to that noise, not sad or angry, but accepting, the golden light becoming more and more pale as the last clouds grew together overhead. But something else, strange and unforeseen, was happening.

117

As the light dimmed, it caught in floating puddles that danced with each other and let fall golden leaves that twirled down like snowflakes, forming into four shining clusters. One of the clusters fell over us, a single gold snowflake touching me, but the rest fell all over Yoona. And the other three gold-clusters fell over the three closed coffins, Zak, Robbie and Denie. They fell and melted like water, running all over the sparkling caskets and seeming to sink inside. The light round me grew pale and dark and Gret and Lis came back to life as their tight golden strings untied. Now the light was grey, except for the glow at my feet and the gold outlines of the three closed caskets.

The outlines melted as we watched. The gold trickled inside the caskets and somehow also melted into Yoona's body. Gret and Lis were free and awake now and as we watched, we saw something unbelievable, something that should not be happening. The rain-crystal lids were swinging open.

For a moment, the caskets seemed full of melting gold snowlight, dazzling a last time up into the pale grey chamber. Then as it shimmered and vanished, we could see the three upturned faces. Lis cried out softly and ran across the chamber to Zak's casket. Gret and I stood there because it was so fantastic, so incredible and we didn't dare believe. Then Yoona's body stirred at my feet and I knelt beside her, touching a warm cheek and seeing her eyelids flutter. At the same time there was a sharp heavy sob from Lis, because the black-haired boy in Zak's casket opened his eyes.

'He's alive,' choked Lis, the happy tears running down her cheeks. 'Reb and Cei, too.' All the life was given by the last golden moments of a dying NUN.

I still don't understand why NUN gave them life. NUN was angry because it had failed to control me, because I broke its bio-code and gave it death. It should have hated all human life, but it didn't. Maybe there was something in the programme that stopped it, but I think there was another reason. NUN had given all these kids life and could not bring itself to destroy them. It had somehow held on to their life-sparks, Zak, then Robbie and Denie, because they were NUN's children. In the very end, it used its last precious drops of bio-energy to restore life.

I still don't know about NUN – about the Graeme-hologram on his bike, about the tall brown-skinned man who was his grandson and who appeared across the NUN chamber, who controlled our lives and tried to control all of the new planet Earth. And when NUN was sighing out its life and truly dying, I hope it heard Lis's happy sobs of joy as she lifted a breathing Zak in her arms. Perhaps even saw the tears on her blue cheeks as she kept repeating, 'They're alive, they're alive.'

Yoona was all right, too. I could hear her breathing, sweet and strong, and in the same moment COL came on-line, humming with power, the *real* COL, freed of its chains. Because life was happening again through the spaceship and the force suppressing COL had gone.

'Systems on-line,' said the super-cool voice as though it had never once thought about blowing us all up. That's computers for you.

Yoona's eyelids twitched again as she heard the voice of her beloved COL. But she was still deeply asleep, because life does not come back easily from near-death. Nor was it for Robbie and Denie. NUN had not only kept the life-spark in their bodies, but healed their wounds; right now they could scarcely open their eyes and they were going to get a surprise when they saw me. Then the little transmitter Gret had on her belt crackled into life. It was Bren from the control deck.

'Gret, anyone, are you receiving?'

'Receiving,' said Gret and there was a sudden cold tension in the NUN chamber because of the tone in Bren's voice.

'You'd better get up here quickly.' The same tone was still there in his voice.

'What is it?' asked Gret.

Lis had come away from Zak and was listening. So was I, because Bren is a tough guy, not afraid of anything. But when he spoke there was fear in his voice. The NUN chamber went even more pale and cold with his words.

'Something's coming up on us.' The fear he was trying to control was too strong. 'Something out of hell.'

13   Doomsday

It was something out of hell all right, and something from
across space – still only a tiny white dot in the distance, but
getting bigger and bigger. Bren flicked the screen to full
magnification and we watched the horrible thing in silence.
It looked like a pitted grey-white ball and quite harmless.
But it was the most terrible monster ever to live in deep
space. It was an ameb.

NUN had mutated trites and amebs out of the Martian
gene bank and lost control of them. Amebs were horrible
things, a cross between an octopus and a jellyfish, fast and
able to crush even a spaceship the size of Deepwater. This
one was just about the biggest, and on Deepwater's second
voyage, it followed the spaceship through the time-warp
back to our solar system. They had freed themselves of it
by taking it too close to the planet Jupiter. Jupiter's
enormous gravity had sucked it down into the chemical
oceans that sweep its surface.

'It should have died there,' whispered Bren.

'Jupiter's oceans are full of methane, ammonia and
hydrogen,' said Gret. 'Somehow the ameb processed that
into food or maybe there were primitive life organisms to
feed off.' She stopped, going pale. 'So it just grew . . . and
grew . . .' She shook her head disbelievingly. 'But to
escape . . .'

Bren was already doing the calculations. Jupiter's gravity
is many times greater than Earth, so to escape the ameb
must have grown and become many times bigger and

stronger. As the results flickered on-screen, even Lis gasped with fear, the first time I had ever heard that sound from her.

The thing coming towards us was twenty times bigger than Deepwater.

'Get a bearing on its course,' said Gret. She was still pale and only whispered, because amebs terrified them the most. And she knew the course bearing before Bren spoke.

'Earth.'

It was bypassing Mars, because even this far out in space the ameb could smell a fresh, living planet, something to settle on like a huge vampire mass, stripping it of life the way you suck juice from a fruit. Then it would get bigger, go to Mars and get even bigger, then out to wherever there were living planets. NUN's mutation from the outer limits of space would become the greatest monster in the galaxy, then hunt life anywhere in the universe.

I knew what had to be done. The others did, too, but I hoped their thoughts did not go as deep as mine. 'How are Yoona and the others?'

'Still practically asleep,' said Lis. We'd brought them back with us to the lower deck. There was a catch in her voice as she went on, thinking about Zak. 'We have to stop that thing.'

Bren flicked down the screen magnification, but through the eye-windows the grey-white dot was now a small round ball. It was coming up at an incredible speed, a huge mutated lump of monster death. 'Half an hour before it reaches us,' said Bren.

'The OMAs are too small,' said Lis. 'But we could reach Earth in a Wingfish.' Yes, they all knew what I was thinking and I hoped again that their thoughts were not as deep as mine.

'Better collect the gene bank and get into our space suits,' I said.

We had only one chance and that was Deepwater itself.

Even if the laser cannon were working, they wouldn't even scratch that thing. The other Deepwater had self-destructed in outer space, in such a colossal ball of sunburst energy, so immense that they heard the explosion, although noise cannot travel in deep space – and so powerful that when it happened, our own Deepwater was thrown aside by the shockwaves, and there are no shockwaves in outer space. The explosion of pure solar energy, generated by a hundred alien suns, created its own rules. I was very scared now, but calm, too, knowing what I was thinking was right. We were in our space suits now and had the precious gene bank. Gret, Lis and Bren went below to help the others into their space suits. I was alone on Deepwater's command deck.

'COL,' I said softly. 'I am taking full control, obey nobody else but me.' I didn't think COL would agree, but it did.

'Yes, Conn.'

COL had used my name. I think it knew what I was going to do and for the first time I felt really close to Deepwater spaceship, like a living part of it, as I went below. Yoona, Zak, Denie and Robbie were being dressed in their space suits. They were blinking sleepily and Denie tried to focus her eyes on me before shutting them again. Here I was, Connal, Meatgrinder, the school bully, and maybe she never expected to see me here. But they were shuffling a little as though coming to life and Gret opened the trap-door that led below to the Wingfish bay.

We helped them down the steps. Deepwater could be controlled from anywhere on the spaceship, but thankfully nobody tried while we went down those steep steps to the launch bay. Bren helped Robbie, Lis led Zak and Gret took Denie. I helped Yoona, our helmets clacking together, her sleepy eyes turning on me as though she knew there was something badly wrong with her spaceship.

Here were the steep steps, where the adult clones had dragged Denie so long ago – months of Deepwater-time, years of Earth-time. There was only one Wingfish left, streamlined with a high tail and two stubby wings: the other was lost on the second voyage, but this was big enough to hold us all.

'Strap them in,' I said.

Lis gave me a puzzled look, but Gret and Bren just got on with it. Even this was unreal, because they were getting ready to leave Deepwater, the home of all their lives, with nothing but the clothes they had on. There was nothing to say goodbye to. Gret climbed in, then Lis. Bren made to follow but stopped, pointing through the port that ran like an iron-glass jaw along the bottom of whale-like Deepwater.

'Look!' he yelled.

The ameb was even closer. But there was something wrong – it wasn't heading for Deepwater, but past it. I knew that would happen; this ameb knew too much about the destructive powers of a Deepwater to come near us. And it was scenting the sweet living smell of planet Earth, even more reason to ignore us.

'COL, set course for the ameb,' I said.

'Ameb moving at same speed,' replied the super-cool voice.

Deepwater's maximum speed was time-blinking, but we were too close for an acceleration like that, even if the ameb stayed still for it. Bren turned to me and saw the look in my eyes. He registered on what I was going to do, but was too late. He was halfway inside the Wingfish and I pushed him hard, even kicked him, I think, at the same time. He tumbled over the control seat and I slammed the side-hatch shut, yelling as I did, 'COL, seal the Wingfish.'

Bren had turned, grabbed for the door handle on his side and yelling soundlessly behind his helmet. I snapped my helmet shut and yelled into the intercom.

'COL, release Wingfish on a course to Earth.'

'Confirmed.'

Gret and Lis were yelling too, just as soundlessly. The

launch bay opened like the lower jaw of Deepwater. I grabbed at hand-holds as the air whooshed round me and the Wingfish rocketed out into space. The two jaw sections came together and I clung as the air and deck pressure returned.

I don't remember running back up the stairs. I was back on the control deck and the ameb was closer. The intercom was open and Bren was yelling.

'Conn, come with us. You don't have to do this.'

'Yes I do.' I hesitated, then without knowing why, said, 'Tell Denie—' My tongue glued on anything else. Just, 'She'll understand.'

'I'll tell her, Conn,' said Lis with tears in her voice.

She understood, and so did the others. There was no other way and any of them would have done the same thing. But they weren't the kid from the eighth casket, the one who could end NUN; who could end life and so had to give his own life. I still hated tears, because I was scared of being weak, so I just said 'Goodbye', and cut the intercom switch. Feeling dead already, I slipped into the control chair. 'COL, I have manual control.'

'Confirmed.'

I'd never fully realised how wonderful that voice was. Not with a sex or with a face, but controlling Deepwater, the most wonderful thing ever built by the human race and in minutes, Deepwater and me would be gone. There was no turning back and I felt the fire of a strong raging pride, because I was doing something *right*, something unselfish that mattered. Something that all the Irish and Rarotongan warriors in my past would have approved of. I couldn't see the Wingfish now because we had turned back, but I was good and ready. Everything was OK.

'COL, set course to intercept the ameb.'

Through the eye-windows, I could see the ameb clearly now; pitted and grey-white as it sped towards us. I think, though, it sensed a living hand on Deepwater's controls

125

because it turned, lumping itself into a monster ball. It was still some hundred thousand kilometres away, but our closing speed was too intense for the thing to escape – it *couldn't* escape, and my Deepwater crewmates and the precious gene bank would be saved.

'COL, intercept the ameb and prepare to self-destruct.'

COL, intercept the ameb and we are both dead. That was what I was really saying. But I had taken NUN's life; Mum and Earth-life were all a distant past and soon I would know what real death was. The ameb was still ahead and in a minute, Deepwater would be too close. Cunning as amebs were, they knew nothing about human nature. Humans will die for what they believe in, and my lips stretched in a tight grin because that was something this ameb would find out too late. We were clear now and this was the moment. One instruction forward and we would ram. Then a voice, silver and sharp, split through my mind.

'Get out of here, Conn.'

A hand grabbed my arm and threw me out of the control chair. Someone was standing over me, a woman, black hair with a bright, good face, but shimmering all over in a silver-sparkling light.

'Chibbi!' I yelled and tried to get up.

Her strong arm threw me down. 'Not Chibbi, her bio-force. Go, Conn.'

'You don't exist, you can't leave COL.'

She gave a real Chibbi grin. 'You broke the programme, Conn, so I changed the rules. Go now.'

She sat freely in the control chair, so much like the real Chibbi, smiling and with one silver-sparkling hand playing over the console. Deepwater turned, centring on the ameb, and I yelled loud and defiant.

'I can't leave. The Wingfish is gone.'

Chibbi's face shone as she looked at me. Deepwater was still turning, the ameb still in sight. 'Yes, Conn, Deepwater is yesterday and you are tomorrow.'

'The gene crystals, activating them—' I yelled.

Chibbi just sparkle-grinned. 'Oh, you'll find the way.'

I opened my mouth to yell again, but she raised a hand and bright sparkling energy streamed from her fingertips. I was grabbed by those sparkling light fingers and pushed away. I saw Chibbi-force a last time, laughing and waving goodbye, as the light force grabbed me more strongly. It was as though the gravity of Deepwater was a rushing river storm, pulling and throwing me down the stairs. I was like a twig over rocks, missing the sharp metal stairs by millimetres as I rolled into the launch bay over the hard metal floor. It was a miracle my helmet didn't shatter open and Chibbi's laughing light force was warm with love round me.

'Bye, my warrior Conn.'

The launch bay itself was rocketing loose. It was a giant escape pod tumbling out of Deepwater, side jets snapping into life and the whole jaw-shaped mini-spacecraft jetting away. Through the iron-glass port, I saw Deepwater turn and head straight for the ameb. I stood up, floating, because there was no pressurised gravity in the craft, grabbing the sides and looking through the port at Deepwater.

'Chibbi!' I shouted, but there was no reply.

Then out of nowhere, like a chill unseen wind, I could hear a song I knew. The words of a folk song that I had last heard on Earth sung by a black-haired young woman strumming a ukelele.

'The olive tree stands in stony ground, but my true love waits beneath it . . .'

She was a young woman who became a force in saving Planet Earth, and the spirit force of Earth's gene ark. Now that spirit was going to its death, singing.

'Goodbye, COL,' I whispered.

The singing went up. Deepwater was moving faster now, faster and faster as it headed for the ameb. Then at the very last minute it drove itself into the monster grey-white mass

127

like a big silver nail. The singing stopped and the intercom went dead.

The ameb turned, humping itself as though it had swallowed something awkward. It seemed to be trying to pull itself inside-out, maybe even split up to lose that big silver death-nail inside. Then it froze solid and the grey turned darker. Lines ran across the mass, blistering into orange-brown cracks; the ameb was burning inside. Now the cracks were black, and opening and from them came the intense white glow of our dying spaceship. All our memories, all our strength, was burning in a fire to save the human race. And from across space, I could see the ameb shudder. It was fighting something stronger and again, across the no-sound blackness of space, I heard a wailing death-cry.

Then suddenly the mass exploded in a brilliant sunburst of energy, scattering black particles in all directions as the fireball closed in on itself and went out. Through my jaw section, I heard the last humming note of a song-beat. Then the last flame-flicker of Deepwater blew out and darkness, as black as dead ash, closed round. Black space was wiping a hand to clean everything, and of the ameb and Deepwater there was no sign.

That was all I remembered.

When I woke up, it was dark. Overhead, a metal monster insect was looking down in silent curiosity.

14 Earth-born

The monster metal insect was part of the jaw section of Deepwater. The iron-glass port was open, I was tumbled out and beyond were lights and movement. By accident or design, the jaw section came down in the same place as the Wingfish. Yoona came up, Robbie and Denie behind her, and they pulled me up. Three pairs of arms, hugging me so tight that tears squeezed out of my eyes.

Gret, Bren, Lis and Zak – they were all there, the complete Deepwater crew together for the first time. I told them what had happened. I had missed my chance to be brave, but Denie just hugged me tight and said in a scolding way not to be stupid. And Robbie grinned and punched my arm as Yoona once did, and it felt better than all the medals in the world.

We all sat down and I told them about the Chibbi-force and the end of Deepwater. They said nothing, smiling at me in a way that was really embarrassing because all I'd done was follow my instincts. We had something to eat and Denie pushed the food up to my mouth as though I were a baby. We were all numb, though, and the ground seemed to shake even though it was solid underfoot, because this was the end of the ride and Deepwater was gone.

Yoona opened the box and tiny jewels sparkled with moonfire. I took one out, pressed its tip and the hologram of a strong hopeful kid smiled at me, burning like a smiling flame in the darkness before going out.

'We still have to make the gene bank work,' said Zak. I

liked him; his skin was a light yellow-brown, he was good and quiet, sitting really close to Lis, and his great dark eyes smiled even more than his mouth. Zak was alive, loving every minute, and Lis was holding him tight.

'And we'll never get back to Mars,' said Gret, pushing green hair out of her eyes, her green hand locked in Bren's red one.

'We don't have to,' said Yoona. She stood up in the darkness, Robbie beside her. 'We were Martians when Deepwater took off, but not now.' Her smile was as strong as ever. 'This is our planet and colour doesn't matter. What matters is being together and making the new life work.' Her golden-brown eyes looked at green-skinned Gret with red-skinned Bren, blue-skinned Lis with yellow-brown Zak, Denie and I red-skinned together. Her words rang up into the black sky and stars.

'We are together. *That* is what matters.'

Her words warmed us better than firelight. We settled down to sleep, pairing off into the darkness. It was warm, black and lovely and I put my arms round Denie as she did the same. 'We can make this work, Conn,' she said softly, but there was still a tiny question of doubt in her voice. All of reborn Earth breathed round us, the last tiny group of humans who had to make things happen.

We slept in each other's arms and woke before dawn. I had been having strange dreams of life, NUN, COL, and all the programming that took us from gene cells into bodies, all round the universe. They were sharp splitting dreams, sparked into each other, flashing like the gene crystals, and as soon as I opened my eyes I saw something.

The lower-jaw section of Deepwater was gone. Even in the darkness I could see that. The distant humped mass of the Wingfish was still there, but the lower section of Deepwater was gone, back into the heavens, either from a programming instinct or a call from above. Maybe it was gone because we didn't need it any more; maybe something not dead had called it up.

Denie sat up and kissed me. I kissed her back. We had the gene bank with us and she opened it, taking out a gene crystal. She traced her finger down the numbers on the side, breathing them. 'Seven sevens. I remember finding this one on the other Deepwater.' She blinked at me with lovely brown eyes, serious and full of resolve. 'But COL or NUN would never tell us how they worked.'

'We were supposed to know,' I said. Denie and I sat up, still holding each other. 'It was in front of us . . . we were supposed to know.'

I ran my finger down the crystal and turned it up towards me. On the end was stamped the tiny NUN symbol, earth, water and fire enclosed.

'Making life,' I whispered.

'Conn?' said Denie, puzzled, then *she* realised, at the same time.

We were by the river. I splashed forward into the shallow water and scooped up mud into a pile, Denie kneeling beside me. Then I put that little gene crystal, stamped 7777777 along its side, into the mud, keeping my hands cupped round it. And straight away it worked because the capsule fluttered like a tiny warm bird and glowed so hotly it was like holding fire in the darkness. I had to let go and it spluttered, the earth and water bubbling round it. We got up, backing off. Denie yelled loud for the others to come.

It was simple. So simple. Whatever hi-tech genius made that capsule also let it be triggered in the most simple way – reaction to earth and water, the mixing elements of life. And we all stood round in a circle and watched because it grew so quickly and with such beauty out of the soil, as though being pulled into shape by gentle invisible hands. In only minutes, the earth model of a human body lay on its side.

Denie pulled up a handful of grass and knelt. She rubbed the grass gently down the body and the mud slicked away, showing smooth skin. She was a young blue-skinned woman, about our age, naked. As Denie softly wiped the face with grass, the eyes opened. They were blank, but by moonlight we saw the life come into them. The lips moved, though not enough to make words, and Denie leaned over to cradle the young woman's head gently in her arms and whisper the most important words heard on Planet Earth for perhaps a million years.

'Be still, this is the moment of life.'

We planted our torches in a big circle round the blue-skinned woman. She knelt in the middle, head bowed and eyes shut again as though all this was too much. I knew how she felt and I knew how important she was. And how innocent. When she opened her eyes, she would believe anything we said because we are the angels who gave her life.

It was awesome. Everything would come from the life-making and the different colours of the human tribe would never again matter. It was too much for all of us, so we split up again; Denie and I stayed by the dying torches with the kneeling blue-skinned woman inside them. We all had to think in our twosomes and work out what to do. The blue-skinned woman scared us, because without speaking she told us our lives as kids were over; we were adults now, in charge of the human race.

Still, though, the dark land round us was beautiful and I thought about that Connal and his mum, so many hundred thousand years before, hoping they reached the mountain-tops together. Connal, that was me, once the school bully and thicko. I must have said that aloud because Denie put her arms round me and simply said, 'Conn, you grew.'

It was near morning now and the others came back. Zak and Lis, Gret and Bren, Yoona and Reb, the outlines of darkness on their pale intent faces showing their decisions. All their lives they would work to make the human race come alive. All of us were still thinking about Deepwater; it was impossible not to. Surely Deepwater could not have survived that explosion, but strangely, we still felt its closeness as though it was somewhere high in the black heavens and would one day return. I said that aloud, too.

'Maybe,' said Yoona. She was the closest to Deepwater and understood it more than any of us. 'We changed the programmes and everything changed. But we can't rely on Deepwater returning.' A soft wind gently stirred the blonde and red hair round her intent face. 'We have to rely on ourselves.'

She was right. I kissed Denie again and didn't care if the others were watching. From the big smiles on their faces, they'd been doing a lot of that too. So we smiled our big grins and Yoona's words stirred us inside like a fire. This time, we were going to make things work.

The kneeling blue-skinned woman had still said nothing, but now moved a little as though coming from deep sleep into a blinking, half-awake unknown life. Now she made a little noise and moved. She was surrounded by torchlight and the angels who gave her life. She made another little noise and her hand twitched, wanting to point. All of us, at the same time, realised what she was looking at.

Not upwards, because there was no sign of our Deepwater spaceship in the dawn skies. Perhaps it was better that way, because our newborn woman had it right and knew what she should be looking at. Not up at the empty sky, but ahead, where she could see a magic sword of red sunrise cutting away the blackness.

Day One on her new Planet Earth.

If you have enjoyed this book,
you might also like books by
CHRISTOPHER PIKE

Last Act	£3.99	☐
Spellbound	£3.99	☐
Gimme A Kiss	£3.99	☐
Remember Me	£3.99	☐
Scavenger Hunt	£3.99	☐
Fall into Darkness	£3.99	☐
See You Later	£3.99	☐
Witch	£3.99	☐
Master of Murder	£3.99	☐
Monster	£3.99	☐
Road to Nowhere	£3.99	☐
The Eternal Enemy	£3.99	☐
Die Softly	£3.99	☐
Bury Me Deep	£3.99	☐
Whisper of Death	£3.99	☐
Chain Letter	£3.99	☐
Chain Letter 2	£3.99	☐
The Immortal	£3.99	☐
The Wicked Heart	£3.99	☐
The Midnight Club	£3.99	☐
The Last Vampire	£3.99	☐
The Final Friends trilogy	£3.99	☐

The Deepwater Trilogy
by Ken Catran

Deepwater Black	£2.99	☐
Deepwater Landing	£2.99	☐
Deepwater Angels	£2.99	☐

All Hodder Children's books are available at your local bookshop or newsagent, or can be ordered direct from the publisher. Just tick the titles you want and fill in the form below. Prices and availability subject to change without notice.

Hodder Children's Books, Cash Sales Department, Bookpoint, 39 Milton Park, Abingdon, OXON, OX14 4TD, UK. If you have a credit card you may order by telephone – 0235 831700.

Please enclose a cheque or postal order made payable to Bookpoint Ltd to the value of the cover price and allow the following for postage and packing:
UK & BFPO – £1.00 for the first book, 50p for the second book, and 30p for each additional book ordered up to a maximum charge of £3.00.
OVERSEAS & EIRE – £2.00 for the first book, £1.00 for the second book, and 50p for each additional book.

Name...

Address...

....

....

If you would prefer to pay by credit card, please complete:
Please debit my Visa/Access/Diner's Card/American Express (delete as applicable) card no:

Signature...

Expiry Date...